T0087746

The Last Days of El Comandante

LATIN AMERICAN
LITERATURE IN
TRANSLATION SERIES

The Last Days
of El Comandante

Alberto Barrera Tyszka

Translated by Rosalind Harvey and Jessie Mendez Sayer

UNIVERSITY OF TEXAS PRESS

Austin

Copyright © 2015 by Alberto Barrera Tyszka
Published by agreement with Tusquets Editores, Barcelona, 2015
English translation © 2020 Rosalind Harvey and Jessie Mendez Sayer
Published by arrangement with MacLehose Press
First University of Texas Press edition, 2020
All rights reserved
Printed in the United States of America

Cover design: Isaac Tobin
Interior typesetting: Cassandra Cisneros
Typeset in Spectral
Book cover printed by Phoenix Color, interior printed by Sheridan Books

Requests for permission to reproduce material from this work should be sent to:
    Permissions
    University of Texas Press
    P.O. Box 7819
    Austin, TX 78713-7819
    utpress.utexas.edu/rp-form

♾ The paper used in this book meets the minimum requirements of
ANSI/NISO Z39.48-1992 (R1997) (Permanence of Paper).

Library of Congress Cataloging-in-Publication Data

Names: Barrera, Alberto, author. | Harvey, Rosalind, 1982–, translator. | Sayer,
    Jessie Mendez, translator.
Title: The last days of el comandante / Alberto Barrera Tyszka ; translated by
    Rosalind Harvey and Jessie Mendez Sayer.
Other titles: Patria o muerte. English
Description: First English language edition. | Austin : University of Texas Press,
    2020. | Series: Latin American literature in translation series
Identifiers: LCCN 2019026435
    ISBN 978-1-4773-1657-3 (paperback)
    ISBN 978-1-4773-2103-4 (ebook)
    ISBN 978-1-4773-2104-1 (ebook other)
Subjects: LCSH: Chávez Frías, Hugo—Fiction. | Political culture—Venezuela—
    Fiction. | Venezuela—Politics and government—1999—Fiction.
Classification: LCC PQ8550.12.A62 P3813 2020 | DDC 863/.64—dc23
LC record available at https://lccn.loc.gov/2019026435

doi:10.7560/316573

For my daughters, Paula and Camila

I can't believe that this is death,
the death of which I speak so much,
from which I expect so much.

—RAFAEL GUMUCIO

The Last Days of El Comandante

The sound of the ringing telephone cut through the night.

Miguel Sanabria didn't hear it. He was in the bathroom, brushing his teeth. Beatriz, his wife, was in the living room, watching television. She shouted out, letting him know that someone was calling without taking her eyes off the screen. The word "telephone" flew down the hallway like a stone being thrown. Sanabria went to answer it. It was his nephew Vladimir; he was agitated, nervous, speaking as if the words were crashing into each other in his mouth. I need to see you, he said. And Sanabria replied: Whenever you like. And Vladimir said: As soon as possible. And Sanabria asked him what was going on. Is it urgent? And Vladimir replied that it was. Very urgent. I'm terrified. I've just got back from Havana, he said. Sanabria said no more.

He didn't know precisely what it was about, but he was absolutely certain that this emergency was related to the president's illness. Over a year ago, on June 30, 2011, a night resembling this one, his nephew had called him just after Hugo Chávez announced on television that he had cancer.

"Did you see him? Did you hear him speak?" Vladimir had asked him.

Sanabria had just turned seventy and had retired from the Institute of Clinical Research at the Central University. He was an oncologist, and had devoted a large part of his professional life to studying and teaching.

Toward the end of his career, he became more and more interested in matters far removed from surgeons and syringes. He set up a partnership with Madrid's Complutense University and laid the groundwork for the incorporation of psycho-oncology as a subject into the medical school's academic program. Time had made him, as it does everyone, more flexible. By the time he reached retirement, he believed that science was not enough when it came to understanding the body.

"What do you reckon? What do you think?" Vladimir had kept asking, stubbornly insistent.

Sanabria didn't know what to say. Recognizing yourself in a disease, calling it your own, it casts an emotional spell. A tumor instantly turns you into a victim. But Sanabria did not want to comment. He needed to avoid giving too much away. He knew that, on the other end of the line, his nephew was on edge, waiting expectantly for his response. They had always had a special relationship, very close, and during all these years neither of them had allowed their polarized politics to destroy this bond. Vladimir was a trusted government official. Sanabria had never voted for Chávez.

He wasn't in the highest of spirits, either. After leaving the university, Sanabria had started to feel more and more unstable. He would often go from feeling anxious to melancholy, and quickly. And just as quickly, he would swing back from melancholy to anxious. Just like that. For no apparent reason, he felt fragile, defenseless. Sometimes he would wake with a start in the early hours of the morning, fearful, as though he had been caught making an escape. Beatriz would be sleeping soundly by his side. Sanabria would then get up and go to the kitchen. He would usually sit on a stool and take a mandarin out of the fruit basket. He could hear cars driving past on the motorway in the distance. He would sit for a while, gazing into the shadows as he tore the peel off the fruit. He noticed how its piercing, citrus scent gradually pushed aside the smell of the night, the smell of the sheets, the smell of that dream he had escaped from once again. Biting into the soft flesh soothed him. Sinking his teeth in and feeling the juice of the mandarin squirt onto his tongue brought with it a strange sense of calm. He occasionally woke up with the inexplicable desire to cry. This began to happen more often. The days when he would wake up in the middle of the night with a feeling of despair stuck in his throat became more frequent. Sometimes he would remain there for a while, hoping that the sadness would pass. He would take deep breaths and then hold the air in his lungs, as if he were underwater. He closed his eyes. He opened them. As if waking up were just like drowning.

At first, he thought that it was a fleeting crisis that had to do with turning seventy, with his retirement. He thought that insomnia was a way of grieving. Gradually he came to understand that he was facing a much greater imbalance. The very thing he had tried so hard to avoid was, at last, happening: the country. Sanabria had spent more than ten years trying to exist on the fringes of reality, avoiding conflicts, trying to prevent what they called the revolution from affecting him. He had resisted all predicaments, family rows, university debates, even his daughter's departure for Panama, clinging at all times to common sense, setting himself apart from the radicals on both sides, regarding everything that was happening as part of a temporary malfunction that, sooner or later, would be resolved, allowing everything to go back to normal. But then came the mandarins in the early hours of the morning, and the inexplicable desire to cry. He realized that he had reached saturation point. Deep down, he was sick of the story. He felt that Venezuela was a mess, a wreck that wasn't fit to be called a country. He believed politics had poisoned them and that everyone was in some way contaminated, doomed to the starkness of picking a side, to living with the desperate need to be in favor of or opposed to the government. It had been too long since they became a pre-apocalyptic society, a nation in conflict, always on the verge of explosion. A cataclysm could occur at any moment. Conspiracies, assassinations, wars, terrorist attacks, shootings, executions, sabotage, uprisings, lynchings . . . Every day a massacre was possible. The country was always on the point of exploding but it never did. Or worse: it was exploding in slow motion, little by little, without anyone actually realizing.

Managing destruction: digging one's nails into a mandarin's peel.

Beatriz's position was far more straightforward: she believed that it was Chávez's fault that Elisa had gone to live in Panama. She thought that if another kind of government had been in charge of the country, her only daughter would not have been forced to emigrate. Elisa and her husband and little Adrián had decided to accept a job offer and had moved to Panama City. They lived on the forty-second floor of a building with a view of the sea and the heat and the humidity, while, in Caracas, Sanabria and his wife learned how to be grandparents through their computer screen.

On the night Chávez announced he was ill, Beatriz felt vindicated.

Sanabria recalled that moment now. As if the call from his nephew had jogged his memory. It seemed incredible to him that it was only a year and a half ago. He felt as if more time had passed. At the beginning of June 2011, Chávez had interrupted an international tour and on June 6 he had gone into hiding in Cuba. The government later announced that four days after that the president had undergone surgery in one of the island's hospitals for a pelvic abscess. The news took the country by surprise. Surprise very soon gave way to bewilderment. There was a strange atmosphere of friction, and the news about Chávez was unclear, even contradictory. The questions multiplied. That evening, Sanabria and Beatriz found themselves sitting in the living room, watching the head of state's message on the television.

"I wouldn't be surprised if it was all lies," Beatriz muttered. "Something the Cubans made up to distract us."

Sanabria watched in silence.

Chávez looked thin and pale. He was on his feet behind a podium, and, oddly, he was reading out a written text instead of improvising in front of the cameras. It was unheard of for this man, so fond of speaking for hours in front of any audience, to restrict himself to a few words, suddenly held hostage by a small piece of paper.

"I don't believe a word of it," Beatriz said.

Sanabria forced a whistle through his teeth, asking for silence. He wanted to listen.

The president said that he had undergone a procedure, they had carried out a drainage; he explained that on June 20 he would have to have another operation, because an "abscessed tumor with the presence of cancerous cells" had been detected.

"An abscessed tumor? Does that exist?" Beatriz asked her husband without looking at him.

Chávez explained that the tumor had been completely removed and that he was now well on his way toward a full and fast recovery. Then he started to talk about the nation and about himself, about himself and about history, about the revolution and about himself, about himself and about Fidel Castro, until he concluded with a new battle cry: "Now and forever! We will live and we will be victorious!"

Beatriz frowned, stood up and exclaimed:

"If it's true, then good, damn it! He deserves it!"

Miguel Sanabria looked sternly at his wife, a reprimand in each pupil.

"Don't look at me like that," she went on. "The guy's a piece of shit and he's done the whole country a lot of harm."

"No one deserves to get cancer, Beatriz."

"That's what you think!" she said, heading for the kitchen. After a few seconds, her voice floated down the hall again: "Maybe it's a punishment from God."

Sanabria shook his head; he hated hearing Beatriz talk that way. He was against the leader, but couldn't bring himself to share those opinions, those attitudes. He was actually quite impressed. Chávez hadn't let any doctors speak, hadn't given any specialists the chance to express their opinion, as would have been the norm in a similar situation anywhere else in the world. Even in his fragile state, he insisted upon maintaining control. He hadn't let anyone deprive him of his starring role. Let alone at that moment, in those circumstances. He had sent another message too, one that made it clear the only voice authorized to speak about his body was his own.

That he was the sole owner of his illness. That he ruled over medical wisdom too, over science, over what could be known and stated about his health. Essentially, he was making it clear that he would continue to set the political agenda, even from inside the operating room.

"Who was it?" Beatriz said, getting into bed next to him, pulling the covers over herself.

"Vladimir."

Beatriz's hands stopped moving and she turned her face slowly toward him. Her gaze revealed a restrained eagerness.

"Does he know something?"

A year and a half later, Chávez's decision to maintain absolute control over what was said about his illness remained intact. On December 8, 2012, he addressed the country to announce that he needed to have another operation. No doctor had spoken, and he didn't quote any medical reports. It was just him, as always, announcing the possibility of his absence for the first time. At that moment, Vladimir was a member of a team of advisers in the president's office. He traveled to Cuba as part of the president's entourage. He was back home a few days later. And the first thing he had done, as soon as he'd landed, was get in touch with his uncle. Surely it had to be something urgent.

"He really didn't tell you anything?" Beatriz asked, before turning out the light.

Sanabria made a vague, bored gesture. He didn't want to tell her anything. Beatriz had been far too anxious recently. Uncertainty only fed her intolerance. The healthiest thing would be to lie to her.

"Vladimir told me it all went well, it was normal."

"Nothing's normal here."

He woke up too early again. It was only three thirty in the morning. He sat at the kitchen table, listening to the cars going by on the highway in the distance and squeezing a mandarin in his left hand.

"We're worried," his nephew had said to him.

The plural is always ambiguous. Who were they? Who was he referring to, exactly? The news about the results of the operation was unclear. Chávez's health continued to be an enigma, and the fact that he hadn't ruled out the possibility of the treatment's failure, the fact that he had chosen a likely successor, added a sense of unease to the mystery. The streets were filled with rumors.

"I need your help, Uncle."

Sanabria had a bad feeling.

"Did the operation go well?" he asked.

Vladimir didn't reply. At the other end of the line there was a pause, the distant echo of a gesture. Sanabria couldn't bear the suspense.

"What do you want me to do? Do you want me to look at some more tests?"

Once before, his nephew had taken some clinical test results to Sanabria, asking for his opinion on the case.

"No, Uncle. This is something else," Vladimir said. It was clear he was nervous. "It's something confidential. Very confidential," he repeated. "Can I trust you?"

Sanabria said that he could. But he felt as if his tongue were being covered in sand.

"What do you need?"

"I need to hide a box."

When he opened his mail, he came across a message that began: "Dear Dr. Miguel Sanabria, you may not remember me—my name is Andreína Mijares, the owner of apartment 34." He did not, in truth, remember her. He closed his eyes and silently repeated the name. It seemed familiar to him, musically familiar. As if it were an old sound he knew but was unable to name. None of that, however, prevented Andreína Mijares from being there, in his email, telling him all of her woes.

"For personal reasons," Mijares wrote, "I was forced to travel to and take up residence in Miami. Unfortunately, things haven't turned out as I hoped and now I'm planning on coming back to Venezuela. Ever since I left, years ago now, I have rented out my apartment to Fredy Lecuna. The thing is, I've been trying to get in touch with him for several months, to let him know I'm coming back and to plan everything properly but, so far, unbelievable as it may seem, I haven't been able to do so. I don't know if I've got the wrong email address, or if the telephone in the apartment is broken, but it's been impossible to get hold of him and now it all seems very strange and is starting to worry me. Thanks to a cousin of mine who spoke to the concierge, I found out that you're now the chair of the residents' association and he gave me your email address. I guess you're aware of the situation in the country. I'm coming back in December, and I need my apartment. That is why I'm writing. And believe me, I hate to bother you with all this, but, as I said, communicating in any way with my tenant has proved impossible. If you could help me in any way, I would be so grateful."

When he retired, Sanabria had accepted the role of chair of the residents' association. He had thought it would be a good way to keep himself busy and do something useful. He never imagined that it would be a particularly demanding job. It was a small building, five stories high, with eighteen apartments and two penthouses. It had a covered open-air parking lot and, at the back, a narrow garden, a kind of gazebo with a bougainvillea to one side that cascaded with purple flowers when in season.

Naively, Sanabria had believed that it was a minor responsibility that wouldn't take up much of his time or give him much grief. He was wrong on both counts. A group of humans contained within five floors of a building can offer several kinds of hell. Up until this moment, they had all been minor. But Andreína Mijares's letter, hanging there in the middle of the afternoon, gave him a sinking feeling.

He knew exactly who the Lecunas were. They lived on the third floor. They were a young couple with one son, Rodrigo, who must have been around nine or ten years old. But he couldn't recall Andreína Mijares. Memory is as arbitrary as fantasy. Sanabria imagined memory like the depths of a dark sea, blue or green, where shadows suddenly slipped by and unknown people or unexpected objects appeared or disappeared. Why had he not retained a single image of Andreína Mijares? Why had he forgotten her? Why did his memory only offer him a gently undulating and immense body of water?

"How can you not remember her?" Beatriz exclaimed. "You even helped her once in the car park; she had a problem with her car."

Sanabria shook his head with vague disappointment. Nothing.

"A short woman, kind of shy," Beatriz insisted.

No. Sanabria only felt the movement of the waves between his ears.

"What about her?"

"She's coming back. Back here. And, obviously, she wants her apartment."

"Well, she's screwed," Beatriz said with reproach. "The Lecunas aren't going to leave. They've got nowhere else to go."

Fredy Lecuna was a journalist. He worked on the crime desk of one of the country's biggest dailies. For years he had been chasing crimes and locking them up in the corner of one of the newspaper's pages. By now he was an expert in the art of writing about the dead: their full name, their age, their marital status, their profession. And then the causes, the reasons: strangled, hit by a car, two bullets, three stab wounds. And the circumstances, of course: living your last days stretched out on a bed in a sleazy motel is not the same as dying in the middle of the street with a gun to your head, a few seconds before your car gets stolen. It always helps to point out some detail in particular: saying that the dead man was bald or mentioning that he had been wearing a pair of mustard-colored pants could make all the difference. You had to avoid clichés, all your typical words. "The deceased," for instance, is predictable. It belongs to the category of monotonous jargon that doesn't grab anybody's attention. Death should surprise language, too.

He was put on the crime desk from the moment he started out as a junior reporter with the paper. At first it was all quite exciting; he even thought that being a reporter was like being a more respectable policeman. But over the years, everything became so tame, including his capacity for surprise, for indignation, for disgust. There were so many murders every day, so many robberies and kidnappings, that he could sit down and pick the one that was most opportune, the one with the most literary possibilities. There were always a few you couldn't ignore, obviously. Like the case of Corporal Diosny Manuel Guinand, who was tortured to death over forty-eight hours in a military center in the east of the country. Faced with this, there was no decision to be made. To compete with such excess was impossible. It was an unparalleled crime.

Little by little, he learned to distance himself, developed a sort of second skin, an inner jelly any shock could bounce or slide off of, something that prevented him from getting too involved with the story. It was impossible to spend every day with a different family that was crying with rage and impotence due to a murder, trying not to suffer with them, trying not to be moved, doing whatever you could to avoid sharing their tragedy personally. It is impossible to be so close to pain and carry on living an ordinary life. According to the Venezuelan Observatory of Violence, 19,336 murders had been recorded in the country the previous year. It was easy to write. Nineteen thousand, three hundred and thirty-six. But it was a terrible figure, one which could be summed up by the horrible fact that, in 2011, fifty-two homicides had taken place every day in the country. Two every hour. The statistics for the current year threatened to be even higher.

There just aren't enough journalists to cover that much blood.

When Sanabria went to see him to talk about the email he'd received, Fredy Lecuna was alone in his apartment. His wife was at work; Rodrigo was at school. It was eleven o'clock on a Wednesday morning, but Lecuna was dressed as if it were four o'clock on a Sunday afternoon.

"I left the paper. I've been out of work for the past three months," he said, inviting the other man in.

Lecuna explained to Sanabria how the group of businessmen who had bought the newspaper had imposed a new editorial line, a different view on what could and could not be news.

"They don't want anyone to talk about insecurity, about violence."

"So what do they want?"

"They want good news, positive stories. It's self-censorship, pure and simple," he grumbled.

When at last they got around to the subject at hand, Lecuna admitted that both he and his wife had been contacted several times by Andreína Mijares: telephone calls from her friends and relatives; emails; even, once, a letter in an envelope that someone had left for them with the concierge. We got it all, he said, but we couldn't reply. We can't. Sanabria understood this was Lecuna's way of letting him know that he and his wife had no intention of admitting they had received the message that he had just delivered, either. Lecuna had his reasons.

"It's hard for us too, Doctor, try to understand. We don't have an answer. We can't give her an answer. It's impossible for us to move somewhere else. We have nowhere to go. Here the rent is more or less affordable; we wouldn't find anything like this anywhere now. Everything is far too expensive. We'd have to leave Caracas. This is complicated, Doctor, you have no idea.

And now I'm unemployed. Tatiana's freelance. She earns a bit here and there as a designer, but that's it. Put yourself in our shoes."

Sanabria listened without blinking. He silently lamented once again having accepted the role of chair of the residents' association.

"We're doing OK here, more or less, struggling, just like everyone else. Because things are getting more and more expensive. Because there isn't enough money. Do you know how much Rodrigo's school is costing us? It's madness. And now this woman suddenly decides to move back from Miami, saying that she has to come back and she wants us out, just like that, by any means necessary. She only says things went wrong, didn't turn out how she wanted. What about us, huh? How is any of this our fault? Are we supposed to just deal with this shit? Do you understand what I'm trying to say, Doctor?"

Sanabria said yes, that he did understand. But he also understood Andreína Mijares. Regardless, the apartment was hers and her return seemed inevitable. He didn't think it made sense to put the matter off any longer; sooner or later they would have to talk to her and find a solution to the problem. The journalist said that there was no solution. That's life. Sometimes problems just can't be resolved. They just stay that way forever. And then Sanabria told him that it was highly unlikely Andreína Mijares felt the same way. And then, before he left, he said again that, unfortunately, they didn't have many options. There was only one: to leave. The apartment was hers, what more could they do?

A few days later, Fredy Lecuna had a revelation. He was lying on the sofa, looking out at the late afternoon sky.

He felt drowsy, but couldn't get to sleep. His gaze was drifting in and out of focus in the air, just about to enter that blurry zone where one is neither asleep nor awake, when, all at once, he was seized by an idea. It was like a neon insect. Shiny and green. The journalist sat up, startled. He thought of desperation. He thought, too, of hallucinations. But the insect was still there, hovering restlessly before his eyes. It was a simple, straightforward, brilliant idea: the solution to all his problems was to write a book.

It was an epiphany. He stood up, feeling almost jittery, and called Gisela Vásquez, an old friend who was on the board at a big publishing house. He spoke giddily, like he was asking for help, and managed to get a meeting with her later that same afternoon.

"I only have fifteen minutes," Gisela told him, before she even invited him to sit down.

Her office was spacious and exuded an efficient, businesslike air: it held a long table, practically bare, with two telephones on the left-hand corner and a large computer screen in the middle, on which a graph was clearly visible. To one side, near the door, stood a small bookshelf on which the latest titles were stacked. Gisela Vásquez greeted him warmly and then took a seat behind the desk. She looked at him, waiting for a sentence, a sentence that would explain why Lecuna had asked to meet her like this, so urgently.

"I want to write a book," he said.

A few seconds went by before Gisela Vásquez smiled mockingly, stood up and walked over to the shelves that stood against the wall by the door. The sound of her high heels rang out, an excessively precise *click-clack* that seemed to drip from her hips.

"Everyone wants to write a best seller," she said, returning with a book in her hand.

She placed it on the table and then turned to walk back to her seat. The book on the desk between them was the third in a series of novels written by Erika Leonard, an English author also known as Erika Mitchell, or E. L. James. In brisk prose that addressed female eroticism, she had achieved a disproportionate amount of success, as detestable as it was enviable for any other writer. Lecuna didn't know what to say. At first, he considered telling Vásquez what had happened that afternoon, how he had suddenly found himself face-to-face with this revelation or epiphany. A shiny, neon-green insect. But then he decided that talking about that kind of phenomenon during a work meeting wasn't particularly professional. He couldn't exactly say that he had had a flash of genius while half asleep, and that was why he wanted to write a book. Then he thought that the best thing to do was to tell her the truth, tell her he'd ended up jobless, tell her about Tatiana and Rodrigo, about the rented apartment they had to leave, the fragile financial state they had sunk hopelessly into. Gisela Vásquez, however, needed no explanations. She seemed to understand the situation perfectly, with no need for details. She put the Englishwoman's best seller into a drawer in her desk, and began to talk about the commercial success a few journalistic books had recently enjoyed. These were not runaway successes, but reasonable ones—it was important he understand the difference. Lecuna nodded, said that he did. He nodded three times in a row, and instead of just saying *yes*, he said *of course*. Without beating around the bush, the publisher suggested he write a book about the massacre that had taken place in one of the country's inland prisons, a fierce battle between gangs that had resulted in the deaths of sixteen people, some of them mutilated. The leader of the losing gang had had his heart cut out and his head chopped off. Lecuna knew the details, had read the reports. His friend told him that the publisher could offer him an excellent advance, the company was sure that a book on this subject would be an unprecedented market success. Lecuna hesitated. He didn't look hugely optimistic. He outlined some of the concerns he had about access to information, the possible risks of getting involved with the various mafia groups fighting for control over Venezuela's jails.

"You could use a pseudonym. It's more common than people think," Vásquez said.

And then she told him about the case of Juan José Becerra, a cult Argentine novelist, who, under the pseudonym of Mariano Mastandrea, had become a millionaire writing trashy books, filling the self-help shelves in bookshops with new titles. He became so famous that his publishers were forced to hire an actor to travel around the world, giving talks and signing heartfelt dedications as if he were the real author. "Mastandrea" became so real that the actor himself ended up being hijacked by the character he was playing and devoting himself permanently to this new life as a writer. It was a fascinating story, one that both men always stubbornly denied. Mastandrea once went so far as to sue a journalist who wrote a piece about the case. Becerra only gave in once, during an interview for an underground radio station. It was in the city of Junín, in 2001. When they touched upon the subject, he hesitated, wavering for a few moments, and then began to talk about something else with a mixture of nervousness and resentment.

Lecuna wasn't convinced by the tale.

"I don't want to publish under a pseudonym," he said. "I've never done it."

The publisher seemed resigned. She drummed her fingers on the desk, thought for a few seconds, then said:

"I also have a project with Zuly Avedaño, the model—you know her?"

The journalist knew who she was but hadn't met her personally. She was a classic model, five feet seven inches of woman, breasts by Dr. Gómez Tejera, a never-ending smile, ex–Miss Venezuela, ex–Miss World, presenter of an early-morning talk show on television.

"We want to do a book called *Glamor for Everyone*. The idea is something classy—you know, fun but clever. Anecdotes from the fashion world, tips . . . We give you the information, you write it, she puts her name on it, and that's it. What do you think?"

Lecuna said no again. He didn't want to be a ghost-writer, either. And anyway, he knew nothing about the subject. He didn't feel comfortable with that kind of style, didn't think he'd be able to write in that frivolous, insubstantial tone. As he spoke, Gisela Vásquez's expression changed into a grimace, deliberately revealing that the little patience she had left was running out.

"I write about reality, not fiction," said Fredy Lecuna.

"Well, that's where you're mistaken: everything's fiction, even reality."

They sat in silence for a moment, awkwardly. Lecuna started to feel that the conversation was over, that this was it, there was nothing else beyond this silence. And then it happened. A bolt of lightning. The enchantment, the revelation came back. Gisela Vásquez's eyes lit up all at once.

"The answer's right in front of us and we didn't see it!" she exclaimed.

"I don't understand."

"What about the president's illness? Why don't you write a book about Chávez?"

That night, in his apartment, Fredy Lecuna poured himself a large glass of whiskey, with plenty of ice and soda. He needed to think. In the depths of the night, the cars went by on the beltway. A little further off, two explosions could be heard. He thought about his job, the profession of recounting death. How many times had he written the word "bullet"? Sometimes, after writing it, he looked at it, entranced. He almost felt like the word was observing him, too. With a certain defiance, as if challenging him. *Again?* How many times had he pressed his fingers down on each one of its letters?

Typing out bullet: b-u-l-l-e-t. Writing death.

Always writing about people who come to an end, people who disappear.

"One more death and I'm taking you out of school," her mother said.

María didn't reply. She almost never replied. She lowered her head a little, nothing more. She was nine years old and in her third year of elementary school. The two of them were in the kitchen, sitting at the little table, eating dinner. Her mother looked at her anxiously. There was a mixture of tenderness and impotence in her eyes. Then she bent her face toward her bowl of soup and ate slowly, keeping the spoon perfectly balanced on its brief journey from the thick *caldo verde* to her lips.

In the living room, the television was still tuned to the news channel. It was always the same, until her mother switched it off before going to bed. This was the apartment's background music. The anchorman had just read out the latest: there had been another homicide in the vicinity of the Simón Bolívar school in the center of Caracas, the man was saying, reminding viewers that it had become a very dangerous neighborhood, in an area dominated by gangs who fought one another for control of drug distribution in that sector of the city.

"You can study here, at home. That way we won't worry so much."

María moved her head a little again, a brief gesture that expressed nothing. She was neither denying nor confirming anything, she was simply establishing she was still there, that in some way she continued to be present, in the conversation, at dinner.

From the living room suddenly came the sound of shouts and a woman crying. It was the victim's mother, describing to one of the channel's reporters what had happened. Her son had just left school when he was shot. He was in the wrong country, on the wrong Thursday, in the wrong life. He was crossing the road oblivious to the fact that he was really crossing a battlefield between two gangs. A shot fired in no particular direction struck him. That was the news. A stray bullet that had buried itself in the boy's right eye. He was called Winston Enrique González Paredes. The woman could barely speak. She was crying, moaning, lowing. It was a raw, immediate wound. María put her spoon down in the bowl. The piece of cutlery looked like a gray animal in the middle of a green sea. A bullet inside an eye.

"One more death and I'm taking you out of school," her mother said again.

María lowered her head. She didn't like kale soup.

Ever since María could remember, her mother's room had been full of eyes. It was her workplace. She spent most of her time there, shut in, sculpting pupils. Her mother was an optometrist who specialized in ocular prostheses. That was what a tiny certificate that hung in the living room stated. María didn't really understand the words, but she knew what they meant. The diploma said that her mother made eyes for a living. Sometimes her mother let her watch her at work. But she had to keep quiet, stay very still, and breathe very slowly. That was the deal. One day she watched her finish off an ocher-colored pupil. It's for a lady who's had an accident, her mother murmured. She worked at a long metal table by the window. She would sit for hours, concentrating intensely. The table was covered in eyes, jars filled with materials, paintbrushes of varying sizes. She only left the room to smoke and to hear the television better, to watch the news up close whenever she thought something important was happening.

The two of them had always lived alone in the same building, in the upper part of the city center, on a little street between Las Mercedes church and Avenida Fuerzas Armadas. It was an old building, three stories high, with no elevator. Their apartment was on the first floor. It was seventy square meters, distributed somewhat carelessly. The kitchen was right by the front door. It was spacious and had a window that looked out onto the building's square atrium. The living room and dining room shared a single space, small and rather narrow. From there, a slender hallway stretched out, leading to the two bedrooms. The bathroom was between the two. It was a dark apartment. Only the window in her mother's room looked out onto the street. All the others faced the building's atrium. Everything was always a bit dark. All shadows and smoke. María didn't like smoke either. It bothered her that her mother smoked. It bothered her that the entire apartment smelled of cigarettes. Her mother tended to smoke in the living room, watching the TV. Sometimes she fell asleep on the sofa. Just for a few minutes. María would watch her and feel that her mother had always been old. Two years earlier, they had celebrated her fortieth birthday. They went to the beach together. They spent the night in a hotel. María had never had so much fun. Everything seemed exciting, new, different. It was the only time she was able, briefly, to imagine her mother as less old. But as she watched her dozing on the sofa, she found it impossible to picture her younger. What was she like, how did she act, what did she look like?

When María looked at old photographs she found it hard to recognize her. The woman she now lived with was nothing like the young girl in many of the pictures. She couldn't make out her hair, her skin, the expression that contained laughter. They looked alike, of course, but they were also very different. It seemed impossible to María that her mother had once been a young woman, a girl. The body's past is hidden underneath the body. A wrinkle is an implacable definition. It lays waste to everything.

Be careful. Don't get distracted. Don't trust anybody. These had always been her mother's favorite mottos. Sometimes María felt as if, when she opened her eyes for the first time, these short sentences were already there, swimming around her, waiting for her. Be careful. Like a primitive litany, the family tribe's most ancient prayer. Don't get distracted. A dull, constant instruction, which came from within the bones of a god who only sputtered threats, misfortunes forever about to occur. Don't trust anybody. This was the whisper of time. Her mother squatted down, next to her, at the school gates, on her first day of kindergarten, took her face between her hands and whispered this to her. María was wearing her school uniform, red shirt, blue trousers, canvas shoes. She was carrying a thin plastic bag on her shoulders. She was three years old and smelled of mango. Be very careful. Other people are dangerous.

Her mother didn't know what to do with her fear. All she managed was to infect others with it. Constantly. Something was always happening, or could happen.

There was always someone describing what was happening or could happen. Every day was a risk. The television said so all the time. Or else there was always a neighbor ready with a story, a tale. María and her mother listened, somewhere between astonishment and fright. One afternoon the old lady who went from house to house giving haircuts told them the following:

"We were on the bus and all of a sudden two thugs got on. One of them went to the back and the other stayed near the door. They took their guns out and started shouting: Give us everything you've got, your money, your phones. One girl had a computer. . . . Everything. I was sitting at the front. I was really scared. I even thought I was going to wet myself. I gave them the notes I had on me. They said to a boy sitting near me, who didn't want to give them his mobile: Hand it over or I'll put a bullet in your face. A few of us passengers were shouting. And then something strange happened. Because the driver suddenly braked. The robber at the front jumped out into the road and ran off, but the one at the back couldn't get out. I don't know how it happened. I just heard some shouting. They said that when the thug was about to get off, someone grabbed him from behind and another person threw himself on top of him. Then everyone was just shouting like crazy. And the driver sped up then, and the bus was going full speed down the road, so fast we nearly crashed. When he stopped at last, there was a strange silence. That was when I was able to look back. The robber was there on the floor, face down. And the blood was trickling all the way down the aisle toward the door. We were all quiet. And we looked at each other. Nervous. Our faces all sweaty. The driver told the policeman that we had all killed him, together. And the officer stood there in silence. Two other agents carried him off. Later, the policeman just said that he was well and truly dead."

María spent several weeks praying that there would be no more murders near her school. Every night, before she went to sleep, as she lay in bed, she would close her eyes and ask for the bullets to stop. The idea of not going to school anymore filled her with terror, it was the worst thing that could possibly happen. Whenever she heard the television fanfare announcing something extra, a special last-minute news item, she would get goose bumps and she could feel small shards of glass under her eyes. She was so afraid. She imagined her future, her whole future, locked up in this apartment. Alone. The two of them alone. Just them. She and her mother. And the smoke. The smoke, too. The blueish cigarette smoke that followed her mother around everywhere, as if it were a delicate, volatile animal. As if it were her pet.

It didn't take long. Inevitably, Tuesday came around and brought with it another body. Halfway through the afternoon, the story broke on television. The door to her mother's bedroom creaked immediately, as soon as the first notes sounded that promised an unexpected news item. María was in her room, finishing off some home-work, and she heard the hurried footsteps, the rasp of the lighter. She imagined the curls of smoke following close behind her mother. She immediately felt the fear, a metallic chill beginning to expand inside her bones. She stood up and went over to the doorway. The reporter was describing something about a settling of scores, about a dead student. And he mentioned her school. And María felt that life could also be nothing but the echo of a gunshot.

"I told you: one more death and I'm taking you out of school," her mother repeated.

A few days later, she followed through with her threat. She told the teachers that they were moving to San Cristóbal, near the border with Colombia, where their only family lived. She managed to get hold of a copy of the curriculum for María's year group from a friend who worked at the Ministry of Education, and she designed a daily plan to continue her daughter's education at home, without leaving the apartment. One of the teachers found out what was going on and went to see her mother, to try to convince her not to do it. María hid in the hallway, listening to everything.

"Do you know how many people are killed in this country every year?" her mother asked.

"How old are you?" her mother asked.

"Do you have children?" her mother asked.

And then she told the teacher that when she was older and had kids of her own and knew what was going on in the country, then the two of them could talk.

There was nothing for it. Her mother's decision was final. María argued, cried, and even threatened to run away from home. It was all useless. The only thing she was able to negotiate was the internet connection.

"You're only nine years old," her mother muttered.

María didn't speak for two days. She barely came out of her room. She refused to eat. Cecilia, her godmother, intervened, and, at last, a computer arrived at the house, followed, shortly after, by an internet connection. And this was how María began to engage with the world via the web. It was also how she met her boyfriend.

Vampiro: How old are you?
  Mariposa: Why are you asking?
  Vampiro: Just to no
  Mariposa: It's spelled "know"

The boy was sitting on the lawn and looked totally absorbed. He wasn't playing, just gently squeezing the rubber ball in his hand. Sanabria saw in his body language a mild and familiar anxiety. He went over to say hello, asked him if anything was the matter, if everything was all right. Rodrigo said no and yes. No, there was nothing the matter and yes, he was all right. Sanabria didn't know how to continue the conversation and he walked down to the bottom of the meager garden. Dusk was beginning to fall. At this time of day, he would occasionally go down to water the garden. It wasn't something he had to do, it wasn't one of his duties, but he enjoyed it. He found it relaxing to pour water over the green plants. All the time he was there, half an hour, maybe more, the child remained in the same position, with the same expression on his face, as if in a trance. Sanabria looked at him out of the corner of his eye, growing more and more curious. But the boy sat there impassive, unperturbed. He thought that perhaps he was projecting his own disquiet onto Rodrigo. Since that morning, since the call from his nephew, he hadn't been able to think about anything else, he had been chewing over the same questions. What had Vladimir brought back from Havana? What did he want to hide? Or rather, what did he need to hide in his uncle's house? And why had he chosen him? Vladimir knew perfectly well what his uncle's political inclinations were. To trust is a blind verb. Could Vladimir really trust him?

In no rush, he rolled the hose back up again and hung it on a metal hook on the wall; he also busied himself more than necessary by picking up a few dry leaves and making them crunch between his fingers, like big butterflies murdered by the sun. Not even this sound attracted the boy's attention. As he headed back to his apartment, Sanabria went over to interrogate the boy again. He asked him a vague question, an "Everything OK?" without too much emphasis. Rodrigo replied in the same way. He said yes or no, it didn't matter, with the same absent expression on his face. Sanabria hesitated for a second, but, in the end, he gave up, said goodbye, and started walking off. And it was then, only then, that the boy's voice rose up above the freshly drenched plants, offering an explanation.

"I've got a girlfriend!" he shouted.

Sanabria couldn't stop a smile from spreading across his face. He turned around slowly and looked at the boy. He hadn't moved, he was still sitting down, but now his face wore a strange expression of joy and embarrassment, pride and sorrow. Those four words were his confession. Sanabria didn't know what to say. He lifted his arm and gave a thumbs-up. He felt a little silly, but it was the only thing he could think to do. The boy repeated the gesture. They both smiled.

Within a few months, and as a result of sharing the solitude of the garden on occasional evenings, Sanabria and Rodrigo had begun to develop a mutual understanding. At least, that was what the doctor thought. The boy made him feel young. It wasn't an altogether bad bug to catch for someone who was teetering on the brink of old age.

"You're entering that bullshit they refer to as the third age."

Antonio was his only brother. He was four years older than Miguel and, from very early on, their paths in life had diverged. As a very young man, Antonio had been active within the Communist party, then switched to a more radical organization, on the so-called ultra-left; he was briefly a guerrilla fighter in the sixties and ended up a few years later embracing the peace process and reintegrating into civilian life. He went to school to become a lawyer, founded a small firm, and achieved significant financial security, but his personal life had always been a disaster. He had moved in with or married several women, but had never been a present father, let alone a moderately responsible one. This was why his relationship with Vladimir had been terrible at first, and then had become fragile and distant as time went by. Only recently, due to the political situation, had it somewhat improved. With Chávez's rise to power in 1999, Antonio's old dreams had resurfaced. The government began rolling out a kind of 1960s-themed amusement park for his entire generation. At times, the country seemed like a space where they could take their nostalgia out for a spin. In the retro atmosphere, Antonio and his peers relished a series of long-forgotten codes. The first thing Chávez resuscitated was exactly that, a language, a way of naming things. He defended Stalin and the Soviet Union, he quoted Mao Zedong and spoke about Gramsci and the organic intellectuals. Having reached old age, Antonio Sanabria began to feel alive again. The revolution was a hard drug, a sort of ideological stimulant, a path leading back to one's youth.

Miguel Sanabria had never given in to this temptation. He considered himself an independent thinker who questioned things, but was absolutely anti-military. His life had followed a less eventful path. He had studied medicine at university, done his post-grad in Chicago, gotten married, and had a daughter, and his life hadn't held many surprises in store. He and Vladimir had always been close and he had always kept an eye on him. Ever since he was a boy. And over time, their relationship had become more loving than the one Vladimir had with his own father. But there was also a veiled tension behind all of their disagreements. They never agreed on anything. Miguel thought there was no separation of powers in the country, that Chávez had developed a personalist, author-itarian model to control the state and its institutions. He questioned the corruption, the lack of transparency. He criticized the ever-increasing presence of military fig-ures in public roles and decision-making spaces.

"This is the same coup d'état they attempted in 1992. The only difference is that now they are doing it from within the government," he would say.

Antonio believed that all these ideas came from a bourgeois understanding of politics. He also thought that most of his brother's arguments stemmed from a right-wing media campaign. He claimed the middle classes lived in a bubble, that they couldn't see beyond their favorite television channels, their neighborhoods, their streets, their houses.

"You have no idea what's really going on in this coun-try. Go pay the working-class areas a visit, Miguel. Go and see where all the poor people live. Go and see for yourself how he's changing these people's lives."

It was never possible to move forward in these debates and they both always ended up annoyed and irri-tated. The only outcome of this war of words was a bad mood. Precisely for this reason, there was an unspoken agreement between them that tended to limit their conversations to other topics:

"I'm serious. At seventy, you graduate as an old man," Antonio said to his brother that day.

Antonio had developed a theory that stated that, beyond the age of around sixty-five, with some variation depending on individual cases, men suffered a drastic, irremediable change: they stopped representing a threat to women. His argument was based on one element: the gaze of the opposite sex.

He claimed that a man felt power when he looked at a woman. In her eyes was a certain amount of fear. You were a threat. This was the game. This was what it was all about. The man was dangerous, a person with desires. Women noticed this straight away. It put them on guard. Exquisitely on guard. This vigilance was an element of the seduction.

Until, suddenly, everything changed, everything was different. Antonio Sanabria had pinpointed this critical change at around sixty-five years of age. It was a subtle but tragic shift. A journey through the pupils and desires of womankind. They slid sadly from fear into endearment.

"And then they start to look at you like you're completely harmless! Like someone who wouldn't hurt a fly!" Antonio raised his voice in exasperation. "You stop being a tiger and turn into a little bunny rabbit, for fuck's sake! You know what I'm saying? This is old age! This is the worst thing about old age."

It was practically the only way they could speak to one another, in which they got to enjoy each other's company as brothers. Evading the present. Avoiding the news. Vladimir also formed a part of their agreement, and rarely came up in their conversations. It was a voluntary silence that Vladimir was also grateful for.

"I assume you didn't say anything to my old man," Vladimir said, as soon as he walked into the apartment. "I don't want my dad to know anything about this."

In his hands was a small cloth bag. Sanabria supposed the box was inside it.

From the moment Sanabria saw Vladimir, he could tell that something serious was going on. Vladimir looked even skinnier than he was the last time Sanabria saw him, maybe only two or three kilos lighter, but it was immediately obvious. It was clear, also, that he had been sleeping very little and badly. A pair of tiny dark bags hung like old curtains below his eyes. He looked scruffy, exhausted. He wore a permanent expression of unease on his face. It was a grimace that Sanabria knew well, he had seen it many times in his life. It was the body's final weakness, plastered onto the face, enduring life's emptiness.

"Would you like a coffee?"

"I'd rather have a whiskey."

Sanabria nodded. He poured out two generous slugs in tumblers filled with ice. Vladimir said thanks, and nodded. It had been a strange December. No one really knew how Chávez was, how his operation had really gone, how serious the prognosis was. The country was a waiting room once again, a hospital corridor where rumors and questions gathered.

After his first sip, Vladimir began to talk. The thing is, Havana's crazy, he said, several times, at different moments. And he told him about groups in conflict with one another, about negotiations, about the increasingly tight grip on information.

"Nobody knows who knows what anymore. Everyone is walking around feeling a bit dizzy. Everyone's really nervous."

Vladimir belonged to a group of civil servants who had begun to be pushed aside, left out in the cold. As the mystery grew, fewer and fewer people were allowed any contact with the sick man. It was the logic of secrecy, and it was clear that Vladimir was resentful. They had sent him back to Caracas without answering any of his questions, without telling him anything, keeping him on the margins. The way he told it, it was impossible to get hold of any information or clues about Chávez's life. His followers, just like the majority of people in the country, depended solely on a few official reports read out on the national channel by the minister of communication. They were very peculiar reports, lacking in information and full of militant language. They offered no facts. They simply demanded faith and devotion. People started to look for any signs or clues on the faces of the high-ranking officials to try and get an idea of what was happening. The news became an exercise in interpreting body language and expressions. Chávez had not appeared since December 8. No one had seen him. No one had heard him say anything. And the country founded upon his voice was disconcerted, it didn't understand what was going on, it couldn't find itself anywhere.

"It's all very strange," Vladimir said in a low voice. "It's as if he's been kidnapped. We don't know anything."

Sanabria kept quiet.

Vladimir faltered for a moment, downed his whiskey in one gulp, then picked up the cloth bag and, as expected, took out a box from inside it. It was a Montecristo cigar box. He placed it on the table. The two men looked at each other. Vladimir had asked that Beatriz not be at home, and so they had waited until the evening, after Beatriz had gone to the cinema with some friends.

"I can't have this at home," Vladimir muttered.

Sanabria looked at the box. He didn't know whether or not to ask what was inside. He thought about it for a few seconds. It might be dangerous. It was a Havana cigar box. It was about the size of a book. You could see it wasn't new. It was obvious there were no cigars inside it.

Vladimir held it out to him. Sanabria took it with both hands. It was hard to gauge the weight: fairly light, but not extremely.

"Aren't you going to ask me what's inside?"

"I was thinking about it. But I wasn't sure if you'd be able, or willing, to tell me."

"Open it."

Sanabria undid the fragile catch and lifted the lid. The scent of tobacco rose up softly, like an invisible cloud. Inside the box was just a mobile phone. It wasn't one of the latest models, nor was it a relic. Sanabria looked questioningly at his nephew.

"It belongs to one of Chávez's personal security guards. He was with him before the operation. The whole time."

Sanabria looked down and peered at the device. It looked like a dried-out insect inside a coffin.

"He gave it to me before I left for Caracas," Vladimir said, lowering his voice. "He told me he had recorded El Comandante."

Sanabria suddenly lifted his gaze and looked his nephew straight in the eye. Vladimir swirled the remains of the ice around in his glass.

"A video?"

Vladimir nodded.

"A video of Chávez," he whispered, in what was almost a sigh.

And then he said that he hadn't watched it. Sanabria looked at him again, surprised. Vladimir looked away, uncomfortable.

"I haven't dared."

Sanabria nodded. He put the lid back on the box and placed it on the little table next to them again. Then he said fine. And he told his nephew he was going to look after it. And he also told him that he didn't want to watch the video, either.

Vladimir followed the words, only moving his head.

Just before leaving, already standing by the door, Vladimir took Sanabria by the arm, thanked him, and gave him a piece of advice.

"Cuban intelligence is going berserk. You know those guys are naturally paranoid."

"What exactly do you mean by that? Do you think they suspect you?"

"It's their job to suspect. They suspect everyone. That's why I'm telling you. Watch out for the Cubans. If one of them shows up, throw the box away immediately. Destroy everything."

Sanabria thought that his nephew was exaggerating. But he agreed anyway. Of course. Whatever you want. It's important to know how to manage paranoia, too. After he'd left, Sanabria went back to the living room and sat down at the table again. He looked closely at the box. Was it perhaps a will? How much life can fit into one telephone?

"Are you writing?" she said scornfully, every time she walked past him.

Tatiana did not share his enthusiasm for the book. She thought that Fredy ought to look for a stable job instead, one that would guarantee them a monthly income. Her financial situation was risky enough for the both of them, since she was paid per job, so she didn't think it was a good idea for Fredy to devote himself to a profession as dubious and unreliable as writing books. Not even the advance had managed to change her mind. The new version of jobless Fredy just heightened her sense of insecurity, which she had been feeling for some time now. They had never legally married, they had nothing of their own, their combined professional instability pointed toward a precarious future, their status as tenants was about to explode into conflict, and all this had to be placed in the context of a country in crisis, its only identity one of uncertainty.

Fredy sat motionless in front of the screen.

He had improvised a study on one side of the living room, a narrow desk near the window. There he tried to concentrate. He had gathered a little information, extracts from interviews, as he tried to figure out what tone the book should have. That was the most difficult thing. He had always found it hard to get going. He sat in front of the computer. He waited for several minutes, wishing that the screen itself would whisper the answers to him. He felt impotent, raging inside, his mood bubbling inside his lungs. He had tried to start with a medical reference, a devastating and unheard-of declaration by a renowned doctor. But no one wanted to speak. Or the doctors who were willing had already done so and their opinions had already been devoured by every form of media imaginable. He had experimented with a diary-like tone, a confessional voice, considering the possibility of writing the book using Chávez's voice, from the perspective of the sick man's stupor and pain. This was the result:

"I can't believe that this is happening to me.

"How was I supposed to know that this mild pain was something so significant, so conclusive? It was pain, nothing more. Just a little pain. Or more like an irritation. Or a twinge. Like when you wake up with a twinge somewhere in your body, in your belly, say, or your elbow, or one of your legs. Or a twinge inside your head, those really are awful because sometimes it feels as if the pain is coming from inside your eye. It happens a lot to night owls who have to get up early. I used to be a bit of a party animal myself, I know what I'm talking about. I remember that sometimes we would go out and serenade girls and drink whatever we were given. Some rum here, a beer there, maybe a little shot of aniseed liqueur every so often . . . We'd all end up pretty thick-headed. But no, this is different. I mean, that wasn't the case when it started. It was very different. Of course I don't know when it began, which day exactly, whether it was morning or evening, but I suddenly started to notice that something was bothering me there, that it started to bother me when I walked, that it wasn't going away. And so I said something, I told my doctor: listen, it hurts right here, and nothing I do helps. And then the doctor started asking me about this and that, like all doctors do, they start asking you questions and what happens is you get nervous, because you start to feel like all these questions eventually are going to lead to a conclusion, and that this conclusion is obviously going to be bad, not bad, terrible; and no one wants to hear anything bad or awful, especially when it's to do with your health; and so what you do, what we all do, almost always, is play dumb to see if the pain forgets about itself, gets better on its own or at least gets distracted for a while. I made this mistake too. I thought: this thing will go away. It's when I'm in a certain position. Or because I slept badly. Or tiredness. Too much work, too much stress, that's all. Until I couldn't stand it anymore. With every step would come an 'ouch.' I couldn't keep pretending, I couldn't keep lying to myself. My body was saying something and I was pretending to be deaf. I didn't want to listen. That was my mistake.

"And then came the operation. It wasn't easy. They had to convince me. At first, I was in denial. I've never liked doctors. If you like doctors it's because you're already sick, I reckon. Because who likes being grabbed hold of and fiddled with, poked and prodded, searched for anything bad wherever possible, eh? That's what I mean when I say they had to convince me. As soon as I heard them mention surgery my guard went up. No way in hell. I don't like that sort of thing. My whole life, ever since I was a little squirt. I've always been afraid of syringes, of hospitals, of surgeons' scalpels. I really hate that stuff. Or when people start talking about anesthesia. The idea of being forced unconscious is awful. Because you think, you always think: What if I don't wake up? What if I'm left somewhere in between, lying there on the bed like a caiman, with my mouth hanging open?

"I saw the needle and the anesthetist's eyes, squeezed into the space between his mask and his cap. My youngest daughter was nearby. Give me your hand, I told her. Yes, Daddy, she said. But don't let go, I said, teasing. No, of course I won't, she said. And I asked her: Are you sure? And she said: I'm sure. I could have talked rubbish for hours, me asking a question, her replying, anything at all, just to avoid them sticking that needle into me. Because I was nervous. Because I didn't want them to inject me. Because I didn't want to be left hanging in the void, defenseless, unable even to dream, because when you're anesthetized you don't even have dreams. The true void, as they say. Nothingness.

"When I woke up, I felt like I was coming out of a hole, a horrible, dim, sticky hole. As if I was inside a cow's guts. When I woke up, or rather when I started to wake up, because it all happened very slowly, agonizingly slowly, I was struggling to understand what was going on. I could see it but I couldn't understand it, I suppose. And all I knew was that I was thirsty, so thirsty. And that I wanted to be somewhere else. Without so many wires, without all the little tubes, without the IV, without all that crap connected to my body. I felt chained up, but with probes instead of chains, chained up with probes, that's it. I heard a voice. I don't know whose. But it was far away. A voice from another world, which was actually this world, because I was in the other one, I was returning from the other world. I heard a voice and this voice said: You must wait. Can you imagine? You're telling me to wait? Do you know how long I waited to become who I am now? But that's what happened. Or that's what I remember, at least. Just those three words. I heard them. Slowly. You must wait. And I stayed like that. Thirsty and waiting, I waited for a long time. Hours which at first seemed like days and then like months, then years and thousands of years, centuries, even. All because I didn't listen to my body in time. That is what I have realized. Your body speaks. It speaks a lot.

"I felt like I was being punished. You must wait. In the worst possible way. In the cruellest, most ferocious way. What I didn't know, what no one really knew, was that this was just the beginning. That the pain wasn't a pain in and of itself but rather the symptom of another more serious pain, deeper down. There are shadows that only a scalpel can see. I found this out later, when they sat down to have a serious talk with me, when I thought that it was all over. They brought tests, diagnoses, strange names, impossible words. They put it more or less like this: when we opened you up, we found something else. And in my head, I thought: fuck! Because it's what you always think. Because that fear is always there. I think that from the moment you're born, it's there. Because we're living beings. Every living being knows it has to die. And that's how the word 'cancer' appeared for the first time. Cancer, carcinogenic, carcinoma. Nothing but c's that got stuck in my throat. Like they were made of iron. And you know what? I had no jokes left. For the first time in my life, I think. I couldn't see the funny side. I went pale. Because dark-skinned people go pale too, believe it or not. And everyone went quiet. Because they'd gone pale, too. And they were looking at me differently. Suddenly I had a realization. Like a lightning bolt. As if I'd been struck by lightning. I started to feel as if I was becoming less of a man and more of an invalid. They are two different things. A man has a future, or at least hopes he does. And I recalled the anesthetist's eyes. And I wanted to squeeze my daughter's hand. And I felt the void again, life which can also be a void.

"I couldn't believe that this was happening to me.

"Betrayal always turns up where you least expect it."

After finishing those paragraphs, he couldn't keep going. It would be impossible to maintain that tone throughout the book. In any case, sooner or later it would become jarring, it would sound fake, artificial. To try and invent Chávez's personal story was tempting but impossible. He needed to tell the story some other way, using another voice. Then he thought of the average citizen, the poorest and most average of them all: someone whose only tool for seeking and finding the truth was their television. And he began painstakingly to search through all the images and declarations that existed on the internet. YouTube as historical discourse. The present moment, refreshed with every passing second.

One of the recordings he liked most was dated August 1, 2011. "Is my new look," the president said in his imperfect English. And he laughed. And all his ministers laughed. This was his style, a key part of his charisma. Chávez knew when and how to make fun of himself or the situation he found himself in. He did this unashamedly, there was never any trace of embarrassment. He relied on humor as a way of relating to people, an effective way of sabotaging remote power rituals. There he was, appearing in public after his first round of chemotherapy, without any hair, totally bald, and joking about his "new look," saying the words in English. Lecuna studied the images on his computer, looking for clues in the color of his skin, his bloated body, in every gesture or movement. Nothing stood out. The president claimed he felt perfectly well, that his disease had been caught in time. And he did, in fact, look well and seem happy. Chávez was once again getting what he most desired and almost always accomplished. To be the absolute center of attention. This was perhaps his true concern, his most secret and not necessarily conscious passion. He wanted to be the axis, the point around which everything revolved. The nation, history, his citizens' public and private lives. And he was achieving it. From the start, he had become everybody's patient. His illness was an enigma that had spread throughout the whole country.

He tried to corner Dr. Sanabria on many occasions. He had by now realized that his neighbor didn't want to talk about it. But journalism is usually a way of establishing an order to one's neurosis. Curiosity is always obsessive.

"You're trying to turn an illness into a detective novel," Sanabria told him once, when Lecuna had just begun to investigate.

"Isn't that exactly what it is?"

"It's cancer."

"Of course. But that's not enough. Where is the cancer? In his pelvis? Could it in fact be in his colon? Or his bladder? Or his rectum? Or in his bone marrow? Could it be bone cancer?"

Sanabria was, as always, restrained. He didn't reply.

"And what stage is he at? What grade? One, two, three . . . maybe four? Is it already metastasizing?"

"It's impossible to know any of that," he said.

"The doctors must know! He's just gone to Cuba

to have another operation! Another one? Why? Is that normal?"

"I suppose his doctors there must know what they're doing."

"What about you?" There was a pause, one second. Sanabria felt a tingle in his hand. "In your experience. Considering everything you've seen in your life. As an oncologist. You must have an intuition, some suspicion."

Sanabria smiled, as if apologizing. And still he said nothing.

After winning the elections, when Chávez announced another trip to Cuba and revealed the possibility of his medical treatment failing to cure his illness, Fredy Lecuna got in touch with all his journalist friends and began a frantic search for a connection to one of the thousands of Cubans living in the country. He started to fantasize about the miracle of coincidences. He thought it was likely that one of the Cuban health professionals temporarily based in Venezuela would be linked somehow to somebody who worked at the famous CIMEQ, the exclusive hospital in Havana where Hugo Chávez was being treated. Lecuna believed that a journalist's methods could include coincidence.

One Saturday afternoon, Lecuna was trying to focus on his writing when he heard his wife's voice from down the hall, telling off their son. Less than two seconds later, Tatiana was by his side: you have to talk to your son. Fredy hated that domineering air she sometimes had, that inflection, the emphatic use of the possessive pronoun when she talked about Rodrigo, as if he were only *his* son.

"Are you listening to me?" Tatiana asked, insistently.

And Fredy said that he was, but that at that precise moment he was trying to write. It was like a red rag to a bull. Tatiana took the bait and got even more worked up. His wife explained that she had just found out that Rodrigo was a member of an online chat group. All kids do that, Fredy said, or something along those lines, without looking at her. And do all kids use pseudonyms, too? Tatiana asked in a tone that was at once sarcastic and reproachful. Fredy looked at her without saying anything. His wife nodded, a grim expression arranging itself on her face.

"He calls himself Vampire—what do you make of that?"

The journalist burst out laughing. The nickname was funny and the alarm false.

Rodrigo came out of his room, brandishing excuses, saying that everyone at school used chat rooms and nicknames. It was then that the sound of the doorbell suddenly rang out between the three of them, the sound joining the chorus of the dispute. Tatiana went to the front door and opened it, mid-speech. Her words instantly froze in her mouth. She couldn't even close her mouth. She looked at her husband. Fredy managed only to cross his arms. He had no idea what to say either. Standing in the doorway was a short woman with a good figure. She was wearing a stern expression. She looked at them with curious detachment.

"Hello. I suppose you remember me," she said. Curt and sarcastic.

Neither Fredy nor his wife replied. They reacted as if they had never imagined that this moment might actually arrive.

The woman leaned down slightly toward the boy.

"And you must be Rodrigo, am I right?"

Rodrigo, embarrassed, whispered that he was.

It was the first time in his life that he had seen Andreína Mijares.

María was lying in the dark, under the covers. Half an hour ago, her mother had finally switched off the news and gone to bed. She always did this at 10:30 p.m.: the television also served as her watch. Before closing her bedroom door, she had gone in to say goodnight to María, who was all tucked in, pretending to be on the verge of falling asleep. Her mother gave her a kiss on the forehead. "I love you" or "I'm so tired" were her preferred parting words. Occasionally she would say both. Then she would shuffle along the hall to the bathroom. Still in bed, María could hear the sound of urine trickling into the water, the roar of the toilet flushing, and finally the peculiar noise her mother made as she brushed her teeth. She waited a few more seconds, then, when at last she discerned the soft click of her mother's bedroom door closing, she quickly got out of bed and sat down in front of the computer. The screen's blue light lit up the room. María fetched from the wardrobe the rag she laid each night along the bottom of the door to fill the narrow gap between the wood and the floor. She didn't want her mother to be startled in the middle of the night, on a trip to the bathroom, by the strip of light coming from her room. She didn't want her nocturnal activities to be discovered. Without the internet, her new life would have quickly become a living hell.

María began to get used to studying alone, to living practically on her own. Her mother had designed a time-table, a rhythm, a routine with homework and exams, rewards and punishments. She created a school inside their home. Her bedroom was the classroom, and break took place in the living room, the constant pulse of the news in the background. Between 3 and 5 p.m. María was allowed to watch one of the cartoons that aired then. But only during those hours. At 5 on the dot, the TV was invariably changed back to the news channel, which broadcast one of her mother's favorite items, a program that was critical of the government and invited members of the public to participate and make complaints, and which constantly pointed out how alarming the situation in the country was. As they listened to it together, María would sit next to her mother in her room, watching her work.

One night she dreamed she was in a long green field and that a man with no eyes was chasing her. She was trying to escape, but it was impossible to run fast through the long, coarse grass. The man was huge and he was naked. Even though he couldn't see her, he was coming after her, getting closer and closer, shouting. Suddenly, the terrain changed and they weren't in a field anymore, and there was nothing green. The ground was covered in tough shells that crunched noisily under her feet. It was even harder to move forward. And the man with no eyes was still following her, she could almost feel his breath on her hair. It ended when María tripped and fell to the ground, discovering to her horror that the shells were dried-out pupils, the floor was covered in old, dead eyes. María woke up in tears but she never said anything to her mother. She thought that the dream would scare her even more.

Her mother had gradually scaled down their lives to the space they shared. Existence felt increasingly like an estate agent's pitch. Living/dining room, open-plan kitchen, two bedrooms, one bathroom. They stopped going to the market on Saturdays, going instead to a little corner shop two blocks from their building. Little by little, the outside world grew smaller. Her mother also went out less. The fact that her entire family lived far away, in San Cristóbal, was the perfect excuse. There was nothing to go outside for. Outside, there was only danger. Outside: threat.

Occasionally Cecilia, her mother's best friend and María's godmother, would come and visit them. She was a talkative, very expressive woman. She always brought a gift. She liked a drink, and would turn up with six cans of beer or a bottle of wine. She smoked, too. Sometimes she would stay late, chatting to María's mother. María thought that when they spoke in hushed voices they were talking about men. Once she heard them talking about her; arguing, more like. María heard their words collide, the bitter tone of the dispute.

"I'm just trying to protect her!" her mother said.

"But there's a limit. You can't bring her up locked away, cut off from the world," her godmother was saying.

"What would you prefer? For her to get shot out there?" Her mother.

"Don't exaggerate." Her godmother.

"We heard shots out in the street the day before yesterday!"

"Fine! But that doesn't happen all the time! And anyway, this is her city, her country, the place she happens to call home!"

"It's a pile of shit! Total shit!" Her mother, of course.

Cecilia's visits always cheered María up. She would

never forget that it was Cecilia who really convinced her
mother that it was necessary to install an internet connection in the apartment. María's mother had refused
at first, she thought the internet was another source of
countless perils. She had seen enough news reports, people even spoke of cases of gangs using the web to locate
people and then rob or kidnap them. She also once saw
or heard a report on the relationship that cyberspace
had with pornography and child abuse. But faced with
the girl's insistence and her godmother's determination
she was forced to give in. Afterward, Cecilia told María
that the two of them had to have a serious talk. "Serious"
meant going with her into her room, shutting the door
behind them, sitting down seriously next to her on the
bed, taking her hand seriously, and saying, also seriously:

"Now don't screw this up."

And she continued to look at her, seriously, of course.
María opened her eyes as if someone were tugging on
her pupils from the inside.

"I'm speaking to you like this because you're nearly
ten now, you're a big girl," her godmother said, by way
of explanation. "But you know how hard it was for us to
convince your mum about this whole thing. That's why
I'm telling you, be very careful about what you do."

María still didn't understand.

"Be careful of dirty stuff on the internet," her godmother blurted out, almost flinching, or more like snort-
ing. She was still serious.

And she explained that cyberspace was full of per-
verts, drooling old men in their pants with unshaven
faces who hid behind their anonymity and could do
awful things to innocent little girls. It was a slightly more

adult version of her mother's mantra. Other people are dangerous. Be careful.

With these words still buzzing in her ears, María typed the word "Butterfly" and entered a site that promoted connection and friendship online. The name just popped into her head. It was the first thing that occurred to her. She liked butterflies. She thought they were graceful.

The first big letdown was Wolf-DXZ, who, during their third chat, asked her if she had big tits and a video camera. PoindexterVII sent her a photo of an enormous, very pale penis. María reacted by hitting the computer's off switch and stifling a shout; she could hardly breathe. She burrowed down into her bed and hugged her duvet, filled with anxiety. Several nights went by before she felt like peering into the computer's murky depths again. She never went back to that website, but she found another one and that's where she met Vampire. She loved the two words he used to label his avatar: All alone. They began to chat. Vampire wrote: My parents are a pain in the arse. And Butterfly wrote back: You haven't met my mum. At first, they just wrote short sentences, but, little by little, their exchange became more fluid. They moved from the chat room to email and started having conversations almost every day, or more like every night. A few weeks later, Vampire wrote: Do you want to be my girlfriend? And María wrote: You've never seen me. You don't know what I look like. Vampire: Yes I do. And Butterfly: You don't know if I'm pretty or ugly. And Vampire: You're pretty. María blushed and smiled. But she didn't know what to say. She felt as if she had twenty fingers on each hand. Practically trembling, she wrote goodnight as best she could. And left. The following morning, María wrote him an email: O.K. Let's be boyfriend and girlfriend. But no photos. A few hours later they wrote to each other again. Their conversation was the same as always but everything felt different. Now they were going out.

María waited for a while until she got bored. Vampire hadn't shown up that night for their online date. She wasn't too worried about it. It had happened before. Sometimes the electricity cut out, or the internet was down. Her mother's cough resounded in the darkness. María switched off the computer and walked barefoot over to the door, removed the rag, opened the door and walked down the hall. Her mother's breathing came and went, gliding through the air erratically, like a weary murmur, as if it weighed more than her body itself. It was a shadow of the sounds she made, slowly spreading through the whole apartment. She coughed again. María imagined her tossing and turning in bed, trying to find a more comfortable position. She heard another noise she couldn't identify. Her lungs, gently complaining. A fragile whistle, fading into the darkness. María felt afraid. And sad, too. A strange sadness.

The following day, when she came out of her room for break in the living room, she found her mother standing by the sofa, dressed to go out. She had different clothes on, clothes she never wore when they were in the apartment. María felt like there was more light in the room than usual. Her mother switched off the television and looked at her, an expression of resignation on her face.

"Get dressed. We have to go out."

María almost fell into her wardrobe. Between nerves and excitement, she struggled to put on her purple T-shirt and blue trousers. She felt she was overflowing, that she had more speed and movement than hands and feet. When she went back into the living room, her mother couldn't help but smile.

"You need to brush your hair," she said.

"I'll do it now," María said, rapidly disappearing into the bathroom.

On the way, she discovered that her mother was taking her to the dentist.

"We can't do everything at home, unfortunately," she explained, as they got on the metro.

Her mother had calculated that it was high time María had a routine check-up at the dentist. She had decided not to tell her about the plan to go out to avoid unnecessary excitement and anxiety. Even so, the girl was restless and beaming. She asked her mother if, on the way back, they could possibly pass by her school and go to a little fruit stand that sold artisanal ice creams that she loved. She wanted the guanabana.

"If we finish early, we'll go," her mother promised, putting her arm around her daughter's shoulders.

María felt that closeness, sitting there in the middle of the train carriage. She saw herself sitting next to her mother, on an ordinary afternoon, and she felt good, really good. This life suited her better.

They came out of the dentist's a little after five. Her mother was striding along, crossing roads to take the most direct route to the metro station. She gripped María's hand tightly in hers, forcing the little girl to skip along frantically as she tried to match her mother's pace. She asked if they were going to go for ice cream. Her mother said, I don't know. It's late. And María said she wanted to see her old school, too. That she missed it. And her mother said it was going to get dark soon. It worried her.

María felt she was walking faster than other people. They were in another gear. She asked again about the ice cream place. Suddenly her mother stopped and looked at her. She peered at her watch, too. Then she bent down until their eyes were almost at the same level. Her eyes were shining.

"We can't today, my love. But I promise we will go this week."

María nodded and her mother stood up and set off again, taking her by the hand.

When they arrived at a street corner very near Avenida Urdaneta, a motorbike appeared out of nowhere. Or that's what it seemed like to both of them: that a bike emerged from within the tide of traffic. It suddenly took shape in front of them, like a wild animal leaping out from the shadows. There were two boys riding it. It all happened in a matter of seconds. The boy sitting behind reached out and grabbed María's mother's handbag, tugging at it. Her mother resisted instinctively, without thinking. The boy punched her in the face. María screamed. Her mother was still clinging to the bag. María screamed again. Then the boy driving the motorbike took out a gun and pointed it at them.

"Are you a fucking idiot or what?" he asked. "What the fuck is wrong with you?"

The weapon made a clicking sound.

"Old bitch," said the boy who was still trying to wrench the bag away.

María had no words or screams left in her. She felt as if her eyes were hurting. Then she heard two shots.

Beatriz had always said that there was only one way to solve the country's problems. She would place the tip of her index finger in the middle of her forehead and solemnly say: a bullet. Just one bullet here. She thought that the greatest mistake made in recent history had been not killing Chávez on time. When he carried out the coup of 1992, or when they attempted to carry one out against him in 2002. Those kinds of mistakes have consequences, she would say, tapping the end of her finger against her forehead. Sanabria hated hearing his wife talk this way. He thought that the president's illness had brought out the worst in Beatriz.

One afternoon, back when it all started, he tried to talk about it with her, but it was impossible. They were reading the newspaper together. It was Saturday, July 23, 2011, and Chávez, in Cuba, had offered people his first report on the progress of his treatment. "I want to inform you that I have completed the first round of chemotherapy, which I underwent over the past few days. This round ended successfully. It's like a bombardment—I call it the atomic bomb against evil." The press release was accompanied by a photo in which the head of state appeared in a red shirt, surrounded by various officials. Beatriz immediately pursed her lips and commented that it was all very strange. And then she talked about one supposed clinical account that claimed that all the official secrecy was down to the fact that the cancerous tumor was in the president's arse. Do you actually get tumors down there? Why would that be? she asked in a sardonic tone her husband found exasperating. They argued, raised their voices, shouted at each other, and Beatriz ended up accusing him of being a pushover. I can't bear the way you sit on the fence, she declared, slamming the door and locking herself in the bathroom.

Ever since that day, Sanabria felt that his relationship with his wife had deflated. He couldn't think of another expression, he didn't know how else to put it. Only the image of a loss of air seemed more or less adequate. There was no more oxygen between them. From that moment onward, he also tried to prevent her and his nephew from running into one another. When Vladimir called him up again in the last few days of 2012, Sanabria made sure to arrange to meet him away from the house. They met in a café on Boulevard Sabana Grande. The situation with Chávez was exactly the same, perhaps even worse. Since his operation, a stubborn silence had enveloped the country. Vladimir asked him about the box, and Sanabria assured him it was somewhere safe, that he had hidden it in a drawer in his study.

"Is everything OK?" Sanabria asked, probing.

"I wanted to tell you something, *tío*. If anything were to happen . . ." His unfinished sentence lingered in the air between them.

"How do you mean? What could happen?"

"I don't know. Everything is strange."

"What are you talking about? Is it something to do with you? Or are you talking about the country?"

"Calm down, *tío*."

"How can you expect me to calm down after you say that to me?"

Vladimir's eyes flickered toward the street and he said nothing for a few seconds.

"Anything could happen here," he said, without looking at his uncle. He paused. He turned his face back toward Sanabria.

Sanabria had a feeling. There were only two days left until the end of the year.

"Has he died?" he asked. He felt as though his lungs were rusting over all of a sudden.

Vladimir didn't answer. He let the pause lengthen, and then he said that the real reason for their meeting was to tell Sanabria that there was an American journalist in the country, a young woman he had come to trust.

"If something happens, anything, she knows everything, she knows what you've got hidden in that box."

Sanabria nodded. But he was still baffled, he had no idea how to handle the suspense.

"I gave her your details. She'll get in touch. Whatever happens, give her the box. She'll know what to do with it."

Madeleine Butler had arrived in Venezuela at the beginning of the year. She had taken a direct flight from Dallas, where she had flown the day before from San Francisco, where she had arrived the day before that from Sacramento to say goodbye to her boyfriend, Erik Bandbridge. The night in San Francisco had been painful. Madeleine had driven to the city in a rental car. After saying goodbye to her colleagues from the paper, she had rented the car, a standard model so that her two big suitcases would fit comfortably in the trunk, and then drove through the rain from Sacramento to San Francisco. She was excited and full of hope. She had been planning the trip for months, had persuaded the paper to give her a period of unpaid leave, had already established contacts, had researched and read everything she could get her hands on about Hugo Chávez, and she intended to put together the most thorough profile of the figure to date. Her plan was to stay in Venezuela until October, for the next elections, and perhaps a few months afterward. Erik had supported her throughout, they'd even planned for him to take a vacation in August and travel to Caracas to spend three weeks with her. That evening, after having dinner at Erik's favorite place, a Greek tavern called Skyro's, they went home, made love tenderly, slowly, touching each other gently, until they fell back, exhausted and silent. She laid her head on his chest and stroked the hair that grew there.

"Will you miss me?" she asked softly, with a childlike pout.

And then the telephone rang.

Madeleine felt a cold chill spread across Erik's skin. Erik tried to pretend it was nothing. It was half past eleven. Who could it be at this time of night?

"Let it ring," Erik said. And kissed her.

Before the answering machine could click on, the telephone fell silent. But the echo of the ringing continued to ripple uncomfortably between them. And then, almost immediately, Erik's mobile began to ring.

"I think it's for you," she said.

"It's obvious someone's calling you," she said.

"Maybe it's something important?" she said.

They both thought of Erik's mother, a fat old lady with failing health who lived in Portland. But Erik pointed out that he had spoken to her that afternoon. Everything was fine. And his mobile soon stopped ringing, too. Erik shifted onto his side to face Madeleine. He put his hand on her hip. She was so white, he thought. He smiled at her and asked if she'd been able to get in touch with Professor Lindholm in the end. Madeleine didn't answer him because the landline began to ring again.

"If you don't answer it, I will," she said, her tone revealing her irritation. Or anxiety.

The two of them looked at each other for a moment while the sound went on. She had a bad feeling about this. She didn't like what she saw in his eyes. She saw faint, evasive terror. At last, Erik sat up and picked up the receiver from the bedside table. He said hello and stood up, straight away, and began to talk in a hushed voice, hurrying to the living room, and once there he walked around in circles, as he told someone off quietly, but it was clearly a rebuke, a whispered shout, a tense scolding. Madeleine could just make out a woman's voice on the other end of the line. And it sounded as if she was crying. It was a girlish, watery voice that tailed away. Like a song from the window of a car driving past. Madeleine got out of bed and walked to the bathroom. As she crossed the hall, she saw Erik standing naked in the middle of the living room, the telephone in his hand, gesticulating. Erik saw her, too. But only for a second. She quickly went into the bathroom and shut the door. She sat down on the toilet, her elbows on her knees, and covered her face with her hands. She felt short of breath.

They had met at the end of 2009 on the beach in Santa Barbara. It was 9 a.m. and Madeleine was sitting on the sand, reading a book. She was visiting two girlfriends there for the weekend. One of them had gotten drunk the previous night and had ended up at an orgy she remembered very little of. She would not be emerging from her hotel room until past 3 p.m. The other was getting some exercise, jogging along the coastline. Erik turned up with a towel and a book and chose a spot near Madeleine. There were seagulls squawking in the sky, very close to the water. A dog with no owner was playfully barking at the waves. They began to talk about books. Erik was reading one about the origins of the Wall Street crisis, Madeleine a biography of Hugo Chávez. She had absolutely no interest in the stock market and its fraud rampage. He thought Chávez was the president of Colombia. That's how their conversation began. In fact, it was Madeleine who did most of the talking. For many years, her father had been the representative in South America of a Dutch company that made electric turbines. Because of this Madeleine had lived in Bolivia for a year, in Peru for two, and for another two in Venezuela. She remembered Venezuela most vividly of all. She was a little older by then and her memory still unearthed random images, or words like *parchita*, passion fruit, that burst in her mouth with an incredible sound. Her Spanish was shaky but functional. This was the origin of her professional interest in the subject. Working on Chávez and Venezuela was also a way of delving into her own history, of traveling toward herself. She was twenty-eight and had never gone back to Caracas. At that point in her life, returning to South America was a fantasy, a distant yet persistent dream.

"Tell me," Erik said, amassing a short-lived ball of sand in one hand, "this Chávez character, is he a goodie or a baddie?"

Madeleine didn't know how to respond. She found Chávez's persona unnerving. Perhaps that was why she was so interested in him, so drawn to him. Her first encounter with him had been in graduate school, when she chose to put together a series of journalistic profiles of Latin America's new leaders for her dissertation. The idea was considered eccentric on campus, but then Madeleine had always been strange, different. That was how she began to get hooked on Hugo Chávez. He was the political leader she studied the most, the one she devoted the most effort and words to. Over time, after all the reading and studying, what had struck her as strange and amusing during that first project ended up becoming the focus of her research. She grew more and more interested in the ways in which Chávez established a relationship with his audience, both on a personal level, which was attested to by many, and a collective one, demonstrated by the zeal of the crowd at all his public appearances and demonstrations. No matter what space he was in, Chávez fundamentally came across as an emotion. When the time came to ask her boss at the newspaper for twelve months' unpaid leave to travel to Venezuela, she had a much clearer idea of who this figure was, or at least she thought she did.

"I want to finish investigating something I've been working on for several years," she told Phil Anderson. "It's about Chávez. It's a personal profile. I want to try to interview him. He has cancer."

Anderson looked at her open-mouthed. He pushed his glasses up on top of his bald head and blinked for a few seconds, as if in his shortsightedness he was searching for some trace of clarity. Why would a reporter from a Sacramento newspaper, about to take the leap from paper to online, be curious about such a thing?

Madeleine tried to explain herself. She told him that Chávez interested her as a charismatic personality, that he was a man who had created a new identity for his country, a new portrayal of the working class and of the power he himself embodied. Anderson told her that he didn't understand a damn thing she was saying. And he asked her to tell him a story instead.

"Journalists don't repeat the news. Journalists tell stories," he declared.

This is what Madeleine told him: One day when Hugo Chávez was a little boy living in the village where he was born (a tiny, isolated place right in the middle of rural poverty), a bishop came to visit. It was a special visit, an important event. For some reason, it had been decided by the village that, between the welcome ceremonies, a child would welcome the monsignor. This was the first time Chávez had held a microphone in his hands. A small, unreliable microphone, connected to a weak, portable sound system. But a microphone nonetheless. He held one in his hands before he held a bicycle. Or possibly before he held a pair of shoes with laces and proper soles.

"Is that it?" Anderson was still looking at her, increasingly surprised and perplexed.

"That's how it starts."

When she came out of the bathroom, Erik was waiting for her, naked, sitting on the edge of the bed. He said something vague about a colleague at work, a Mexican woman called Cinthya, who had crossed the border years ago, fleeing from a fate which was the desert or an abusive family, or prostitution, or drug trafficking, or all these things at once and more, much more, the desert, rough sand baking in the sun, the dry earth containing more bones than prickly pears. Erik spoke as if they had talked about her before, as if she were a mutual friend of theirs, with familiar ease. But the damage was done. At least that was what Madeleine thought. She thought there was more to it, that that was obvious. And she wondered if it made any sense to argue, make a scene, fight about it. He would deny everything. She would ask him to at least have the guts to admit it. It's obvious, she would repeat. And she would repeat the sequence, too, evoking the sound of the telephone, the conversation, the way he had gotten up, answering the call at last, running into the living room to begin whispering nervously. He would say no. She would say yes. They would be mired in this argument all night. Was it worth it? She looked at her two suitcases stacked up in a corner of the room. She saw her underwear scattered on the bed. Erik stroked her hair, kissed her forehead, asked her if she was tired. They had to get up very early to go to the airport. Madeleine nodded and burrowed under the covers.

Her seat on the plane was 16D. She flew to Dallas, and there, four hours later, she boarded the plane that would take her straight to Caracas. She had thought about taking advantage of the stopover to call Charles Lindholm. He was the author of a book that had been a huge revelation to her. It was probably the best study on charisma she had come across. It was a serious, rigorous analysis of "the charismatic phenomenon and its relationship with human conduct and social change." She was so excited after reading it for the first time that, after looking up his details on the University of Stanford's website, she had written the author an email, praising his book and briefly telling him about her project. A few days later, in a courteous, friendly tone, Professor Lindholm had replied. They exchanged a few remarks about the Latin

American president. Lindholm told her that, along with another academic, he was researching the subject. They arranged to speak on the telephone when she was ready to set off. Madeleine had left the call to the last minute. She planned on calling from the airport, to use some of that dead time in Dallas. But she couldn't do it. She felt as if there were a dead bird inside her chest. An animal covered in dry feathers wedged within her body. She couldn't stop thinking about Erik, about what had happened the night before, the woman's distant voice, her boyfriend murmuring, her boyfriend blurting out his strange story about the Mexican desert. It all gave her the awful sense of an ending and yet she hadn't been capable of finishing it, of saying the words. Instead she had chosen to slip underneath the conflict, to keep going, as if nothing had happened. I love you, Erik had said to her that morning, before kissing her on the mouth. See you in August.

She spent those four hours in the Dallas airport sitting with Charles Lindholm's book. She drank two lemonades and marveled once again at the writing, this new order that allowed her to give shape to her own thoughts, structure to her impulses, sounds for what before had been only mute intuitions. The flood of speculation she had gathered over the course of her investigation suddenly appeared on the pages of the book, almost perfectly organized, with dazzling clarity. Lindholm understood charisma as a relationship and, using Max Weber's first reflections on the subject as a starting point, proposed that it was only possible to understand how charisma worked by observing the devoted ecstasy of the masses, the bewitchment of the faithful. Faced with this, charismatic protagonists had to constantly adapt and transform themselves for every new auditorium and situation.

She had underlined and bookmarked this quote: "The charismatic leader must search for spectators in their need to fill their inner void, they must set them alight with their zeal, and drag them into their imaginary world of absolute power." Page 94.

To read is to search. To read is to search for oneself. Always.

Deep down, Madeleine also wanted to understand her own bewitchment. What the experts believed to have close ties to narcissism, a sort of borderline personality disorder in which chameleon-like abilities and empathetic powers could turn an illness into radiance, was for her an ardent, dazzling beacon. How had this figure seduced her so easily? How could a distant South American leader seem so irresistible to her? As she sipped her second glass of lemonade she remembered an anecdote, one she had heard from a Venezuelan television producer with whom she had exchanged a few emails more than a year and a half ago. During the 1998 electoral campaign, the then-candidate Chávez went to be interviewed for a television program. Shortly before they went on the air, he reminded the presenter of something that had happened years before, when the interviewer had hosted "Miss Venezuela," the country's most important beauty contest: an identity ceremony. The scene had taken place in Maracaibo, just after the jury had made its decision. Suddenly, three armed forces paratroopers had dropped out of the sky, carrying a gift for the country's new queen. According to Chávez's confession, he had been one of them.

Madeleine had laughed.

And she smiled again as she recalled the story, with a glass of iced tea in her hand, a few hours before touching down in Venezuela. Every time she remembered this story she was amazed by it. Mainly because she couldn't help but also remember the number of times when, in different contexts and circumstances, Chávez had referred to those years and evoked a radically different self-portrait: that of a rebel soldier, secretly working toward the revolution from within the army, camouflaging his combative spirit, listening to Fidel Castro's speeches at night, broadcasting from Cuba. How could these two experiences coincide? How could one be, at the same time, both frivolous and heroic? One of the two stories had to be a lie. Or was it perhaps possible that both were authentic? Who had Hugo Chávez been, and who was he now?

It took her a week to rent a room. It was the best solution, she had been assured, if she wanted to spend a significant amount of time in the country. She had entered on a tourist visa and still wasn't sure how to resolve the question of her legal documents. She was certain, however, that she could not live in a hotel for several months. Especially not in Chacao, one of the quietest, safest neighborhoods in the city, but also one of the most expensive. Thanks to a foreign correspondent she met a journalist whose mother was renting out a room. It was in a peaceful building with a great location. The room was large and she was allowed to use the fridge, the washing machine, and the tumble dryer. Madeleine moved in on a Tuesday. It was January 24, 2012, and Chávez was speaking on one of the state channels. She unpacked her two suitcases, put her clothes away, and felt happy. The sense of having her own space, with a window facing the mountain, gave her an extra dose of optimism. The first thing she did was to connect to the internet. She wanted to let her parents know she had arrived, and to write to Erik and send him a few photos of the room. She had already told the woman who owned the apartment that her boyfriend would be coming to visit her in August. She had a double bed. Her arrival in Caracas and the passing days had gradually buried the telephone call from that night in San Francisco. Madeleine preferred it that way. As she connected, she watched the president on the little television in her room. He looked fat. The whole process of his illness and treatment had affected his image. He seemed a little slow, maybe. But he was still himself, he still spoke in the same way. The cancer didn't seem to have affected his pride, his fascination with himself. If anything, he seemed ever more convinced of his own greatness.

"To love Chávez is to love your country," said Chávez.

Madeleine quickly scribbled down the phrase.

Then she opened her email and was pleased to see a message from Erik.

"Dear Madeleine, there's something I didn't know how to tell you the last night we spent together."

"Hey, kid, are you Fredy Lecuna?"

The voice had an unmistakable Cuban accent. The journalist had been waiting on a corner of Avenida Nueva Granada for half an hour.

Getting there, to that moment of that afternoon, hadn't been at all easy. The Cuban presence in Venezuela was a delicate subject and, like everything else, enjoyed very little transparency on the government's part. There was no official record, no publicly available information on how many of them there were and what exactly they were doing in the country. People knew about the medical, sports, and cultural operations, but nothing else. In an unexpected act of deference, the government had handed over management of the national identity card system to Cuban officials, as well as administration and control of the commercial registries and public notaries. However, it was said, and there were even formal complaints to this effect being presented in the courts, that in almost all ministries, including the armed forces, there were Cuban consultants present. It was at once laughable and tragic. It was inexplicable.

Fredy Lecuna invested a lot of time and effort following his intuition, the hunch that he'd be able to find a Cuban who could secretly introduce him to a medical contact on the island. It turned out to be a rather complicated undertaking. Mainly because Cubans seemed by now to have fear hardwired into their genes. A journalist friend who had written an article on the subject

put him in touch with an ex-nurse from Holguín who, a
year and a half ago, had escaped on a commercial flight
from Maracaibo to Miami. Lecuna called him. The man
named a few conditions, but in the end agreed to talk,
always via the computer, changing his account each time
and without using any kind of camera. Lecuna was surprised by how effective this fear was. Even after everything that had happened, even though he had his North
American documents in order and lived on a spot somewhere on the northeastern coast of Florida, the man was
still terrified. He was terrified of being overheard, found,
caught up with by the invisible specter of the state.

Later on, when Lecuna met Aylín Hernández, he
found it was the same way. He had to tread an arduous
path, pass various tests, prove that he would not put her
in danger. He was put in touch with her by an old class-
mate of his from his journalism course who worked for
one of the government-controlled media outlets. She
was more radical now than when they were both students. Fredy led her to believe that he was working on
a piece for a British magazine and was trying to give a
balanced view of what was happening in the country.
That was how he got hold of a name and a telephone
number. At the other end of the line he heard the voice
of a woman with her guard up, friendly but ever cautious.
Fredy knew this wasn't going to be straightforward, that
it would require a great deal of tact and patience. He had
seen it before: Cubans in Venezuela were practically
imprisoned and were very closely watched. They had to
follow a set of specific, rigorous rules of behavior. Their
relationships with local people had to be strictly professional; any exchanges outside of work were considered
"excessive relationships with nationals" and could lead

to some sort of sanction. There was also specific legislation that allowed the island's government, its police, and its security forces to act in Venezuela as if they were on Cuban territory. Fear proliferated uncontrollably. Like metastasis.

Fredy spent weeks convincing her that he wasn't in the least bit dangerous, that he wasn't going to get her into any trouble. He never hid the fact that he was a journalist, but he told her he was writing an article about how Cubans were doing their bit for the country. Nor did he try to get any information out of her at first, to avoid coming across as an impatient interrogator in search of a scoop. Over the course of several calls he gradually began to gain her trust, until the woman finally accepted his invitation to lunch. Tatiana would have been happier had she been a man, a doctor or a paramedic, not a woman, doubtless a young one, with God knows what intentions. She didn't like his relationship with the Cuban woman one bit.

"Don't be prejudiced, Tatiana."

"I'm a woman. I know my gender," she replied.

In fact, Fredy Lecuna didn't know much about Aylín either. He knew that she had been born in Camagüey and was a voluntary IT worker for the health projects run by the Cubans in Venezuela. That was it. Of course, at two in the afternoon, under the blistering overhead sun, he could imagine one or two other things. He was probably waiting for a thirty-two-year-old dark-skinned woman with firm breasts and a killer sway of the hips. It was then that he heard from behind him:

"Hey, you, are you Fredy Lecuna?"

He turned around, surprised to find himself face-to-face with a woman of about forty, pale and a little chubby, with thick-rimmed glasses and straightened hair falling to the right side of her face.

He took her out for lunch at a Chinese restaurant on one of the streets in the Los Chaguaramos housing estate. They sat at a table in the back and chatted away, relaxed, their conversation wandering aimlessly. Fredy had no clear idea how far this encounter might actually get him, but it was the only different and original idea he had. He had harbored the secret hope that she would be a pediatrician, a graduate of the University of Havana, who would be able to nudge him, even by chance, toward some direct link, a contact who worked at Cuba's Medical and Surgical Research Center, that exclusive safe house where all the secrets regarding Hugo Chávez's illness were kept.

Aylín was thirty-eight years old, and had a mother and two children who still lived on the island. The decision to come and work in Venezuela had been entirely a financial one. As long as she was in the country, the government would give her family the equivalent of fifty dollars a month. Besides, in Caracas, the national authorities paid for her accommodation and she received a monthly stipend of around two hundred dollars, converted to bolívars at the official exchange rate. On the black market, this money just evaporated. According to the agreement made between the two countries, the Venezuelan government paid the Cuban government a total of three thousand dollars a month for each island worker placed in the country.

"They give you 10 percent of your salary and keep the rest," Fredy murmured. "Marx could have written a whole other manifesto about a deal like that."

Aylín frowned.

Fredy thought that it was a crude, modern version of slavery. She thought it was an opportunity to get ahead. A great opportunity. That was all she cared about. Everything she did was in order to support her two daughters, a girl of seventeen and another of fifteen. Working in Venezuela, despite the difficult circumstances, allowed her to get hold of things that were unimaginable on the island.

"This December, for instance, I want to get them each a mobile," she told Fredy, showing him a picture of her two girls.

But as a Cuban, Aylín wasn't allowed to visit the shopping malls. Neither could she get an account with a Venezuelan telephone provider. Her migration status did not allow her to establish any relationship of this kind. She needed someone she could trust, who wouldn't rob her—something that had happened to her and to other Cubans before—someone to whom she could hand over all her savings and who would buy her two mobile phones, a well-known brand, the latest models, one in black and one in silver.

"So, kid, how do I know I can trust you?"

At the publisher's they were getting worried about the deadline. The book had to be finished before the inevitable occurred. Every week, Fredy Lecuna would get a call inquiring about how it was all going, asking if he had some advance copy they could read, how many pages he had written. An editor must chase. They have paid for words that do not yet exist but that they know are there, close by, and they do not plan to let them get away. One afternoon Fredy got a call from a certain Señor Guevara, head of marketing.

"We have information," he said, his tone serious, "that things might happen earlier than we imagined, if you see what I mean."

The journalist thought that death almost always occurred earlier than people imagined. No one ever dies on time. Chávez had already been operated on. The rumors were tainting the Christmas period with a strange surgical atmosphere.

"We don't have much time," Guevara insisted. "I don't know if I'm making myself clear."

Lecuna suddenly remembered when, in July of that year, Chávez registered his candidacy for the elections and declared, "We are jumping from one miracle to the next." The crowds roared, euphoric. "And I am sure that, with God's help, we will continue to live and continue to prevail," he added. To some people, his declaration of intent to win a new election was the best possible diagnosis, more irrefutable proof that he had overcome his health problems. To others, this was just another demonstration of the president's expert impudence. Even though he was aware of his precarious physical state and his abysmal prognosis, he was irresponsibly throwing himself into a new electoral battle.

On the final day of the electoral campaign, the sky opened up above Caracas. Chávez performed the ceremony in a torrential downpour. He was wearing a little raincoat and waved to people as he stood in the rain. The images were filmic. The sequence seemed to have been written. As if the rain belonged to a prepared script, a script about the epic tale of a hero who is going to die.

Chávez won the election on October 7. On the 10th he was sworn in, and, during the same ceremony, he named a new vice president. It all seemed to adhere to a predesignated schedule. Out on the street, as people celebrated, a singer positioned on a stage shouted that Chávez would be president "from two thousand and thirteen until two thousand and forever." He hadn't invented anything new. The phrase was part of a tune that the president himself had started singing a long time ago. "As long as my body can bear it" was one of his slogans about how long he was going to remain in power.

As long as my body can bear it.

As long as my body can bear it.

As long as my body can bear it.

He had repeated it so many times. With such faith in the future. With such faith in his body.

And all his followers had repeated it just like that. Perhaps Chávez's greatest triumph lay in having established his voice as the basis of power, as society's axis. He had created a state that spoke, a state that was also ecclesiastic. Everyone repeated the words of the messiah. It was a perfect structure because it was a voluntary, jubilant exercise in subjugation. There were no questions, just enthusiasm. A great deal of faith. Blind devotion. *Chávez forever.*

Aylín gave him the money inside a black plastic bag.

"Don't be an asshole and rob me," she said, only half joking. With a shadow of a plea flickering behind her pupils. Fredy put his hand in the bag. There were a lot of creased or unevenly folded notes inside. They looked like they'd come from a shipwreck. The two of them were alone in an office belonging to one of the journalist's friends. Fredy counted the bills one by one, laying them out on the desk. It was the exact amount necessary to buy the mobile phones the woman wanted to give her daughters. He looked at her, moved. She was risking everything: her savings and even her legal status. She could end up penniless, and she could even be arrested and deported by the Cuban secret police. And all for a gift, for two simple phones. All for her daughters.

Motherhood is a form of madness.

The journalist took advantage of a special Christmas offer and bought the two mobiles. He gave them to her a day before Aylín was due to travel back to the island to spend the holidays with her family. The woman didn't try to hide her delight. She embraced him. Fredy Lecuna had passed the last test, the final exam. They had a beer.

"Hey," she said after taking a sip and smiling broadly, "now I can tell you."

"What?"

"I found someone. I've got you a contact in Havana."

Fredy sat there, paralyzed. She smiled again. It was only December 14. Chávez had just been operated on and the country was on edge. The effects of his farewell were still being felt. The president's goodbye had been full of doubts.

"I'm serious. It's someone inside CIMEQ, would you believe? I swear."

And then the journalist felt like hugging her, giving her a smack on the lips, leaping into the air in celebration. But Aylín moved her hands, a brief cautionary gesture.

"Hold on, now, that's not all. This thing is about give and take. I help you, you help me, understand?"

Fredy Lecuna thought that her gesture corresponded to what he had already done for her, buying the two mobiles.

"I don't understand."

The woman looked at him, slowly. She seemed nervous, indecisive.

"What do you want me to do?"

"I want you to help me get off the island."

Fredy looked at her, perplexed, trying to figure out exactly what this phrase meant.

"I need you to marry me."

"Nothing's the same here, my friend. Forget about the country we once knew."

Carolina Troconis pronounced her words in a very particular way, gently biting off the ends, dragging out some of the vowels. This was the telltale cadence of upper-class women from Caracas. Carolina was a typical girl from a well-heeled family. First she had studied at a school run by French nuns, and then at the Universidad Metropolitana. She had married, fittingly, a boy from an equally well-to-do family, who over a year ago now had fled the country. He had been on the board of directors of one of the many brokerage firms that had been seized by the government. Ever since then he had been at a spot on the map between Colombia and the United States, waiting for things to calm down, while she had stayed behind to look after the family and their properties in Caracas. This was how she had started working in property. She told Andreína all this as they drank their first vodka, by the pool at the Altamira Club. The sun was sinking into the water, which steadily glimmered. The two women wore sunglasses. This was the first time they had seen each other in at least twelve years.

"Not since María Fernanda's wedding, right?"

They had gone to school together and had kept up their friendship sporadically after that. As they ate, Andreína told her friend about her failed marriage, the misfortune of having married a man without ambition, whose only show of initiative in his entire life had been running away to Maracaibo with his secretary.

"At least you didn't have children."

She told her, too, about escaping to Miami, about her failure in Miami, how she had come back with her tail between her legs and her self-esteem at an all-time low. Eventually she told her about the problem with the apartment. Carolina listened to it all carefully, punctuating the story with a couple of sighs here and there, a few small winces of heartfelt solidarity. At the end, after wiping her lips with a cotton napkin, she came out with two concise, direct sentences:

"The problem is the boy. Minors always make everything more complicated."

"What does that mean, exactly? That I can't make them leave my apartment?"

"It'll be very difficult, if not impossible. They'll try to seek protection from the law, in any way they can."

"But it's my apartment! And it's my primary home! I have nowhere else to go!"

"What can I say?" Carolina raised her eyebrows, proffering a sarcastic smile as she moved her fingers to trace a pair of quotation marks in the air: "Remember we are living in revolutionary times."

"So what do I do, then? Just sit here twiddling my thumbs?"

"The best thing would be to negotiate with your tenants. Couldn't you do that?"

Andreína remembered their first encounter. As soon as they saw her, Fredy and Tatiana stopped dead in their tracks, engulfed in a highly charged silence. The little boy noticed it straight away. Something out of the ordinary was happening. He watched her with surprise, but without the rush of adrenaline bubbling in his parents' eyes. She had wanted to be polite, but she felt so outraged. She had spent too long trying to get in touch with them without getting any kind of response. This prolonged silence had eventually turned into a ferocious battle cry within her. That was the consequence. She had a tightly coiled flame on her tongue, ready to let fly. She harbored a deep hatred for her tenants. Above all, she hated this moment, this situation, having been forced to go all this way, all the way up to this moment when she was standing in the doorway, looking at them, a bitter fight now the only remaining possibility.

Tatiana said: "Rodrigo, go to your room." And the boy went to his room. Fredy said: "Hello, we didn't know you were back." Andreína just asked if she could come in. The other two said that she could, while their bodies naturally moved closer to one other, slowly, as if gradually building a defensive structure, a new parallel body prepared to confront an invading force. They sat down in the living room. Tatiana offered Andreína a coffee, but Andreína asked for water. As the couple went into the kitchen to get it, Andreína's eyes quickly scanned the space, trying to recognize her territory, recover her memory, spot any defects, irregularities, alterations. A few images flashed across her mind. Images of her wedding to Jorge. Her, naked and walking around the living room, unable to sleep, waiting. This memory brought back feelings of vulnerability, but she did not waver. She began with a complaint.

"I think it's unacceptable that you haven't replied to any of my messages," she said.

It was an airport sentence. She had concocted it as she waited in Miami, developed it over the entire journey, and polished it as she waited for her suitcases to appear on the carousel at Simón Bolívar airport.

And then the two of them looked at one other, as if each was waiting for the other to respond. Neither of the two, in the end, offered her an excuse. They chose to let silence preserve the sense of ambiguity. Andreína expected, at the very least, a small show of courtesy, an exercise of pretense that was the usual etiquette in cases such as this. They couldn't even give her that. Her second sentence came out all at once: Andreína asked them when they could move out. The couple looked at each other again. Then Tatiana clasped her hands together and let out a rounded sigh that slowly deflated until it reached the floor. And she began:

"I don't know how well informed you are about the situation in the country, Andreína. Things aren't easy. High inflation. No jobs. Unless you work for the government, of course," she added. "And with this new tenancy law, no one wants to rent out their apartment anymore. It's all very complicated," she continued, as her husband nodded with a precise rhythm at the end of every sentence.

And Andreína replied that she knew perfectly well how things were. But that that was not her problem.

"I informed you both some time ago that I was coming back," she explained. "This is my house, I have nowhere else to go."

Tatiana's smile tightened. It now appeared even more false. Like a faint sketch that was about to transform into a monster.

"I can give you two weeks," Andreína said.

"Two weeks?" asked Tatiana, the sarcastic tone in her voice now evident.

Fredy, sensing a storm brewing between the two

women, tried to mediate, uttering a vague phrase, aimless and useless, something like "I think it would be best if we discussed this calmly." Totally innocuous. The three of them looked at each other. And the conversation began to speed up. Andreína said: I'm sorry, but I've been calm for long enough. Tatiana said: Well, you're going to have to stay that way because we're not leaving. Andreína raised her voice. Tatiana shouted. They both stood up, gesticulating with their hands and threatening each other. Each ordered the other out of the house. Rodrigo came out into the hallway, awestruck. Fredy seized his chance and made Tatiana take the little boy back to his room, then tried to negotiate with the owner of the property.

"We're not going to reach an agreement like this," he said.

"I don't want to reach an agreement, I just want you to leave," Andreína snapped.

"Perhaps it's best to let the lawyers sort this out," said Fredy, opening the door.

From the invisible depths of the apartment's bedrooms, Tatiana's resounding voice rang out:

"Tell that lunatic she better go to hell or so help me God, damn it!"

Fredy gave her a strange smile, a look that said, I know this woman, she means it. Andreína walked out of her house, trembling. Filled with rage, with impotence, with fear. A shudder can be many things at once.

"No, I can't negotiate with those people," Andreína replied.

"Are they Chavistas?" asked Carolina, wrinkling her nose a little.

"Not as far as I know. She definitely isn't. When I first met her she'd just got back from a march organized by the opposition and she was bad-mouthing the government. They seemed like decent people. That's why I leased them the apartment."

"Decent people." Carolina moved her chin distractedly for a second or two, as if chewing on those two words. "You don't know the half of it . . ."

"Tell me."

"Do you remember Memela Aranguren?" Carolina pulled her seat closer and lowered her voice. "She went to our school, two or three years above us."

"Yes, I remember her. What about her?"

"You won't believe this!" She dragged her seat even closer and began to whisper: "One day she comes up to me, charming as you like, asking if I could find her an apartment. She tells me she and her husband sold their house in Valle Arriba, for dollars, you know. They were looking for an apartment to rent. They wanted to be tenants. So I find them a luxury apartment up in La Castellana, the upper part, a knockout place, marble floors, a view of El Ávila, bathroom with a jacuzzi . . . It had everything, Andre, everything, and all brand new, totally lavish!"

"And what happened?"

"Eighteen months later, the owner calls me and tells me that Memela is refusing to pay the rent."

"No!"

And Carolina says yes, a yes with a nod and a hand gesture.

"No!" Andreína said again.

"At first I thought it was a mistake, I told the owner not to worry, to calm down, that I'd sort it out. And you know what, I call Memela and that shameless woman tells me it's true, that she doesn't plan on paying anymore."

"I don't believe it."

"Well, wait, I'm not finished yet. Memela starts talking about a new law that Chávez had passed, or was going to pass. Just listen to this. I couldn't believe it. That bitch, a millionaire who hates the government, tells me that according to this new law she could eventually own the apartment."

Andreína felt dizzy all of a sudden. She said no a few more times. And it was true, she couldn't believe what she was hearing.

"And she's still there. And she won't pay. And she got lawyers involved. It's hideous, darling."

Andreína was mute. Pale.

"And I could tell you about four or five more cases like this, exactly the same. That's what I meant when I said 'decent people.' This country ran out of decent people a long time ago!"

When they said goodbye, Andreína felt empty inside. She waited for a taxi outside the entrance to the club. She felt she had come back to find a different country, a land she didn't recognize, where she was, irredeemably, a foreigner.

"I've known people to chain themselves to their properties to get their tenants to return them," Carolina had told her before she left.

"And? Did it work?"

Her friend made a doubtful face.

"I'm afraid I don't think it'd work for you. The problem is the boy," she repeated, like a litany. "Minors always make everything more complicated."

María didn't leave the apartment for several days. She could still remember what had happened with exceptional clarity. As if the image of that moment had chased her back to the building, as if it had followed her up the stairs. Hurrying. Crying. Shaking. She stopped for a few seconds outside the front door. She couldn't control her fingers. Her eyes stung. She could sense that hot image, breathing down the back of her neck. At last she managed to put the key in the lock. She almost felt like she was drowning. She leaped inside, desperately inhaling the apartment's shadows. She slammed the door behind her and let herself fall, she sat on the floor and screamed. She gave sound to her tears. And hung her head between her knees. And discovered that the image was there. That it had sat down in front of her and was looking at her. That it wasn't going anywhere. María ran to the living room and switched on the television.

It all happened too quickly: her mother was shot twice. The first bullet pierced her abdomen, rupturing her pancreas and taking out her left kidney. It emerged from her back and buried itself deeply in the pavement. The second entered her right cheek, shattered the roof of her mouth, and then broke free, leaving a trail of brain matter and hair. It took only one second. In a flash of two explosions. María froze. Her mother collapsed right away and the two attackers disappeared on the motorbike. María bent down, her mother's body was lying face down, she tried to touch her, it was all happening too

fast, everything was moving faster than she was. Lots
of bystanders came over, bent down, shouted, called for
help. María saw a swirl of words above her. She wanted
to run away. She wanted to be at home. A hand pulled her
firmly upward, then she was on her feet, on the sidewalk,
face-to-face with an old woman who was looking into her
eyes, agitated. Do you know her? Is she your mother? she
asked her several times in a row. The questions felt like
shots, too. María was scared. She was confused, dizzy.
She just shook her head. Without knowing why. Perhaps
out of fear. She just moved her jaw, ever so slightly, from
one side to the other. No. And looked down. Soon they
left her alone and they all went back to the body. That
was the last thing she could remember. A chaotic mass
of people, growing bigger and bigger, swarming around
her mother's body. A Ferris wheel of murmurs and excla-
mations. And the sound of a siren, an ambulance or a
police car, she doesn't know. Just a sound growing closer,
licking the streets. Then she began to run.

Run: her sandals slapping against the ground. Slap
or thwack or crack or scratalack. The air tripping over.
Her tongue dryer by the second. Her heart ricocheting
around her chest, harder and harder. Running. Running.
Running. Terrified.

She entered the building without looking at anybody.
She ran up the stairs, too. Until she stopped in front of
the door. Her door. Her keyhole. And she couldn't control her fingers. And her eyes were stinging. She let herself fall into her apartment.

For the first few days she stayed on the sofa, barely moving, her back straight and her left hand gripping the
soft arm of the old piece of furniture. She never figured

out how she managed it but, although she was looking straight ahead, her left eye was alert to the door, to the outside corridor. Expectantly. At the slightest noise, or the echo of the slightest noise, her pupil trembled slightly. Her right eye, meanwhile, was pointing toward the television, switched on as always, on the same channel as always, showing the same programs as always. Whenever the news came on, this iris would also register a brief quiver. She drank hardly any water. When she was hungry she would go into the kitchen and open a packet of biscuits. One night she heard the far-off sound of some cats meowing. One long vowel stretching out into the darkness.

One morning she woke up and felt dirty. She had fallen asleep on the sofa. Everything was the same, intact. Her mother was nowhere. Not on the television, not at the door, and not on the telephone, either. Her eyelids hurt. Her eyes were dry. María curled up on the sofa, even more tightly than before. She wanted to carry on sleeping, to stay like that, coiled around herself, her hands folded in toward her body, until something finally happened. She wasn't sure what, but something had to happen. She had imagined a knock at the door and her running to open it and there stood her mother, clean, a little disheveled, but clean, with a bandage wrapped around her forehead, smiling. Did I scare you? her mother would ask, before embracing her. She had also imagined opening the door to find two tall men, very tall, too tall, so tall that their heads nearly touched the ceiling and, from up there, they looked down at her as if she were an ant. We're policemen, they declared. Are you María? She also thought that the telephone would ring. But it never did. María began to notice a gaping empty space inside her. It was as if there were nothing in there except the cold. She didn't understand how her mother could disappear like that, without it mattering, without anyone noticing. No one had realized.

   She slept badly, waking up constantly. Her face hurt from crying so much. Her mouth hurt inside, too. She was dizzy, confused, she didn't know what to do, who to call, where to go.

   Butterfly did not dare tell any of this to Vampire. It didn't occur to her to use the computer. She was too defeated, disconcerted. She didn't even know how to react. Knowledge of death destroys initiative. María was paralyzed. She stayed this way until the shock and the pain ended up becoming her new natural order. It is impossible to live with intensity all the time. Sooner or later, fear or anxiety triumph and become routine. A few days after what had happened, María couldn't bear it any longer and decided to leave the apartment. She quickly pulled on any old dress. She put on her tennis shoes. Brushed her hair a little. And took a deep breath. And opened the door. And felt dizzy. Out in the corridor was the sea. The rest of the building was an ocean, a dark, invincible ocean, its waves vigorously swaying, as if the wind were pulling at them. She shut the door immediately. She thought that it was all a hallucination. She thought this with another word because the word "hallucination" was not yet part of her vocabulary. She opened the door again and saw only the corridor, the door to the apartment opposite, the stairs. There was no water but she noticed a subtle scent of the sea. Out on the street she had the same sensation of fear that not even the sun and the wind could ease. She walked along, looking down at the ground and taking swift, short strides. As if she were sliding instead of moving. She wasn't walking: she was fleeing.

She didn't really know what she was doing. She was just following an inner impulse. She thought that perhaps her body, in its desperation, wanted to move, to do something, anything, anything at all, to go and look for her mother. She was afraid. She moved her small eyes around wildly, she felt everyone was looking at her, that everyone knew her story, that in the middle of the street anyone might stop her, grab her, take her by the arm and shout, Here she is! Here she is! She's come out from her hiding place! She's here! She imagined all of a sudden that lots of people began to gather around her, pointing at her, hounding her, Aha! Where did you disappear to? What have you been doing all this time? Why are you dressed like that? Where's your mother? What have you done with her? The voices crowded all around her, flying through the air, cornering her. María gripped the little bag she had come out with tightly beneath her arm. Her steps became shorter, almost little jumps, as if she were a bird.

When at last she stopped, she realized she was near the corner where it had all happened. She felt as if her heart might jump out of her chest. Her hands were cold, her shoes hot. She looked at the sidewalk, the asphalt, heard the sound of the motorbike once more. The memory appeared before her. In brushstrokes. She relived the surprise, the shots, the shout, the fall. Just as she thought it had been. Just as she had imagined it.

"What's the matter? Are you lost?"

She couldn't hear the voice next to her very clearly. She couldn't quite make out the words. They were just noise. And she got scared. She jumped. It took her a few seconds to recover. The sun stopped her from being able to see anything other than the figure of an older man, silhouetted by the dusk, bending down toward her.

María said no. Several times. Nervous. No and no and no. Everything is fine.

Distressed, she set off back home again. She didn't stop until she found herself once again in front of the door to the apartment. Just like on that day. She walked so decisively, looking only straight in front of her, not listening to anything, as if her body knew the way by heart, as if the walk home formed part of a blind, fierce instinct. She was sweating and struggling to breathe. She struggled too to find the key in her little bag. When her fingers found it, when they touched the metal's cold skin, only at that moment, as if this small gesture had opened up some inner floodgate, did María start to cry. She was unable to contain herself. Her sobbing was distraught, it controlled her movements, made her sink down, prevented her from putting the key into the lock properly. She ended up sitting on the floor, her back leaning against the wood of the door, gasping, howling. No one heard her. No one came out to see her.

Gradually her breathing calmed down. The tears stopped. Only then did she hear a voice inside the apartment. She stood up immediately. She felt stirred by a warm energy. It was a distant yet familiar sound. Her hope returned in that moment. She imagined her mother walking around in the living room, faithfully followed by her blue smoke. She opened the door and it took only a few seconds for the hope to crumble and for her to realize that the television was on.

It was December 8, Chávez was talking about cancer. He sounded like he was saying goodbye.

María closed the door. She sat on the sofa. And she closed her eyes, too. Briefly. As if she wanted to switch off the world.

"Chávez isn't going to die. The whole thing is a media trick. You'll see."

This was how his brother Antonio had put it. Unequivocally. They had gone for a walk in Parque del Este and had ended up arguing and fighting. Now Sanabria was lying in bed, next to his wife. He had the remote control in his hand and was flicking from one channel to the next, looking for news, some new information. Several days had gone by since the operation and still he had heard nothing. The silence had turned into a kind of violence. For more than ten years, Chávez had reestablished the state and the country as a system that only functioned with him at its center, pronouncing his name. The possibility that this center might fail, disappear all of a sudden, evaporate or vanish, kidnapped by the night, by that routine natural chaos that is the night, triggered a state of sheer bewilderment in everyone. People's nerves were increasingly frayed.

"Has Vladimir told you anything?" his brother had asked him as they began walking. Antonio wanted to know if his son had told Sanabria anything about Chávez's illness.

"Since the two of you are so close," he muttered, with a hint of reproach. "And since you're an oncologist," he added, in the same tone.

Miguel said that he hadn't. Antonio quickened his pace.

"I think Chávez is as right as rain. I think he's already been cured."

"There are things that don't have a cure, Antonio."

"That's what the opposition wants. For him to die. But Chávez is going to disappoint them once again."

Miguel ignored the comment and tried to concentrate on the blue sky, how its color began to fade at the mountain's edges.

"Since they failed to beat him in any election," his brother pressed on, "they tried to assassinate him."

This theory came from the president himself. Over a year ago, on December 29, 2011, at a military event honoring the armed forces, Chávez toyed with the idea that the cancer he was suffering from had been induced. He found it suspicious that five of the continent's leaders had the same disease. He speculated that perhaps the United States had developed a secret technology that allowed them to transmit the illness in a direct and personalized way.

"It's clinically impossible," muttered Sanabria.

"Don't be naive. The gringos are capable of that and a whole lot more!"

Miguel stopped. The two brothers looked at each other. They weren't out of breath.

"Do you really want to talk about all this today?"

They were silent for a few seconds. Then they started walking again. The blue of the sky was by now giving way to the orange streaks which heralded the end of the afternoon. Antonio kept looking ahead and continued chewing on a few phrases. A few minutes later, the two brothers were caught up in another row.

"You can say what you like, Antonio, but some things

are just unacceptable. Like all that rotten food, what the hell was that all about?"

He was referring to the more than 120,000 tons of foodstuffs, imported by the government, that were never distributed and that went bad in state-owned warehouses and storage facilities.

"No one is held responsible, nothing happens. And the whole thing was a scheme, corruption, pure and simple. More than one person made a fortune."

"The same thing happened before," Antonio grumbled.

"Give that crap a rest, will you? What does it matter what happened before? Or do you mean to tell me that it's the same old shit with you lot as with every previous government?"

Antonio had noticed how, over time, his brother's moderate tone had gradually become frayed, giving way to a more turbulent, enraged frame of mind. He seemed more irritable recently, less tolerant. This attitude triggered an immediate resistance in Antonio. His brother was right. There were unjustifiable things. But it was necessary to defend the government.

"It's not the same shit. This is different. This process is on the people's side. It's the businessmen who corrupt the government officials. The whole thing is the legacy of capitalism."

"Oh, come on!" Miguel felt annoyed again. "Let's try to have a serious conversation! Don't give me that bullshit!"

"This is a long process, Miguel. It's not easy to make changes in this country."

"Do you know how much money has been received these past few years in payment for oil?"

Antonio stopped. He looked defiantly at his brother.

"More than a billion dollars!" Miguel, as he kept talking, took a few steps forward, circling around his brother. "Where the hell is it, for fuck's sake? Look at the public hospitals. Look at the schools. Look at the roads. Look at the economy. . . . Tell me! Where has all that money gone?"

There was a heavy silence. Miguel realized he had gotten carried away, he was wound up. He, who never lost control, suddenly found himself making a scene at the edge of a park. Antonio looked at Miguel sternly, walked over and brought his face right up to his.

"That money is in a place you don't see. It's gone to people who have always been invisible to you lot. In the slums, out in the countryside. The money's been spent on the people, on the poor."

"Don't bullshit me, Antonio!" Miguel felt the heat rising up to his ears again. "You know that's not true! They have no shame. They've turned the poor into a money-making scheme!"

Antonio carried on walking to the rhythm of a compulsory hike. "Next you'll say they didn't steal before!" he grumbled sarcastically.

Miguel caught him by the arm.

"The country didn't work before! And we always criticized it. The difference is that you, now, are incapable of criticizing what's going on. You can no longer see things clearly, Antonio."

They looked at each other for a moment or two, hesitantly, as if deciding whether it was worth persisting with the dispute. They both seemed out of breath, unable to keep up with the speed and heat of the debate. Each took a deep breath. Each looked at a different tree.

"You need to understand, Miguel," Antonio said after a pause, calmer now. "What's going on here is a war. The gringos and the oligarchy are refusing to give up their privileges, and all day long, using every means at their disposal, they are trying to stop the revolution. That's what's going on."

"I see it differently, Antonio. This is all just another wasted opportunity. It's more of the same. With another mafia, other groups, other narcos, but it's more of the same. Look at the army. Look at our leadership. What conclusion can you draw?"

Antonio felt terrible again. He hated that his brother brought this up at every opportunity. He felt like the walk in the park was a hijacking. He wanted to leave.

"We've gone back in time," Miguel said. "We've gone back to tyrants. To military rule. This is our history. The best investment you can make in Venezuela is to carry out a coup. That's the conclusion. Now they're all millionaires, they've got the power, they do what they want."

Antonio shook his head, his expression one of resignation, as if to say that arguing was pointless, that to keep talking would be absurd.

"I don't want to talk about this with you anymore, Miguel. Get it into your head. It's impossible. You and I don't live in the same country," he muttered.

He took a few steps, stretching his legs, as if dispelling a cramp. Then he looked at his brother again, sadly, and added:

"Honestly, I never thought you'd end up so squalid."

The history of language has not registered the moment when the term *squalid* began to be used to describe any Venezuelan who opposed Chávez and his plans. There is no doubt, however, that it was the leader himself who came up with this association during one of his lengthy verbal performances, putting the term on the map. Ever since winning the presidency, Chávez had devoted himself to attacking any form of dissent. An adversary was an enemy. He would disparage them harshly but mockingly, too, with sarcasm. He turned political condemnation into a humorous act. When he said "squalid," the echo was immediate. His followers began using the word with scornful passion, and, little by little, the word was established in the country's lexicon. There were radical groups who defined themselves as anti-squalid. A comment, depending on how in line it was with a hostile attitude toward the president, might be considered squalid. And on the side of dissent there began to be a squalid pride, too. Beatriz took great satisfaction in being ultra-squalid. She would even announce it loudly, tactlessly. When she and her grandson wrote to one another on the computer, she would try to teach him anti-government slogans, something that Sanabria felt was as squalid as you could possibly get. Chávez continued to amuse himself by using the term unreservedly. In April 2010, addressing the nation on a channel that broadcast on all forms of media, he claimed that "being squalid is a disease." And then he started talking about "squalids." "Those who get involved with squalids are headed down the road to perdition." And he assured his listeners that it was a serious disease. For which there was perhaps no cure.

That night, lying in bed next to his wife, looking for some news on the television, Sanabria regretted the fight with his brother and reproached himself for having succumbed yet again to a pointless diatribe.

"It's impossible to discuss anything with Antonio," said Beatriz. "All Chavistas are fanatics."

Sanabria admitted she was right, but the phrase might work just as well the other way around. At that very moment, Antonio could be thinking the same thing about them. At its core, it seemed like a problem of faith. Chávez had taken advantage of his illness to turn politics into a religion. He had already demonstrated that winning elections was what he did best, but throughout that entire period he had been busy with another campaign. He wanted to earn a place in heaven. He turned the disease into a new challenge. An opportunity to become a legend.

On January 13, 2012, as he presented the Data and Accountability Report for the previous year before the National Assembly, the leader spoke without interruption for nine hours and twenty-eight minutes. It was his way of defying all those who doubted his health, anyone who thought he was not in a fit state to remain or aspire to remain for much longer at the head of the government. How was it possible for an ill or dying man to talk for so long without a break? How was it possible for somebody who was weak, fragile, unsteady, decaying, and without a future to exploit the alphabet for such a long, long time? His loose tongue was the real news. His determined tongue, unbeatable, dominating his entire body, dominating even the cruelest frailties of his body, the consequences of so many rounds of chemotherapy, the need to pee, the pain in his knees. His tongue controlling everything, invading maps, suppressing enemies. His tongue: his government.

The country was once again the kingdom of the spoken word. The old legend of El Dorado, forged in the fire of the Spanish conquest, gave rise to a fundamental tradition: history is born of stories. Fantasies are our statistics. Invention is more powerful than the facts.

The disease had made Chávez stronger. He could break his own record of long days of discursive gymnastics and deliver a monologue of almost ten hours in front of the country's media. The proliferation of the media was a sign. The repetition of his word was a symptom of life. The excess of words seemed like a sign of health and was also, in a way, a diagnosis for the country: a territory where a single story ruled. Chávez's suggestion of a new narrative for Venezuelans had been successful. But when he got to power, he began to consolidate this narrative as a new national consensus, with a hegemonic proposal based on his persona, his voice, his tastes and his habits, his preferences and his whims.

Sanabria had spent the whole year closely observing this process. He knew Chávez was lying. Was he lying? At times, watching him on TV, Sanabria felt doubtful. Chávez seemed so sure, so convinced, so honest, so vitally honest. But, on the other hand, Sanabria himself had seen the tests, knew the treatment the man was undergoing. He found it impossible to believe that Chávez didn't know exactly what stage his illness was at, how serious it was. What if Chávez was being tricked? What if he was being lied to? In any case, when it came to the people, the lack of transparency was total. Most people knew very little, and the little that was known was vague, superficial. This cloak of ambiguity and silence continued to grow, building on a major rumor mill. Throughout 2012, the number of oncologists in the country, both professional and amateur, multiplied. Everyone had an uncle or a cousin, or the friend of an uncle or cousin, who in turn had a brother-in-law who apparently knew all about it, had secret information, reliable sources. In the face of the government's discretion or cover-up, a well-known journalist ended up becoming the source of the most accurate information about the president's health. In his newspaper columns and his social media accounts, he would offer concrete facts and make announcements that were later proven to be true. Official sources were only an echo, all of them repeating the scarce information Chávez offered up without adding anything new. Vladimir had told him in strict confidence that specialists from a clinic in Brazil had analyzed the case and had claimed that the treatment Chávez was receiving in Cuba was thirty years out of date.

"Thirty years—can you believe it?"

"He chose it," said Sanabria. "He chose to be a sick man with no doctors."

At a certain point, he had considered the possibility of being treated at the Syrian-Lebanese Hospital in São Paolo, but the institution had refused to accept the security demands, the most notable being the absolute discretion, the vow of silence that the doctors would have to take regarding the president's medical process. Why did he do this? Sanabria wondered. Why did he decide that secrecy was more important than his health?

Chávez won the election and established himself as the messiah. He wasn't really aiming for the presidency. He wanted to win something else. To what extent had he followed this path consciously? Had it all actually been a precise, perfectly designed plan? Sanabria had trouble believing this. The body does not respond mechanically to that kind of undertaking. The other face of illness is miracle. Chávez didn't seem a man prepared to give up easily. And less prepared still to give up on himself, on his success, on his fame. But he was ending his year in silence, mute, imprisoned in a hospital in Havana, once again.

"Is it normal to spend so much time in intensive care?"

"It is. They've already said there were complications."

"But it's still strange, isn't it? He usually loves to go on and on. Now he's not saying anything."

"He can't say anything."

Sanabria had already decided that, as soon as his wife left for Panama, he would open the cigar box Vladimir had given him. He couldn't resist any longer. He wanted to switch on the telephone and watch the videos of the president. It made no sense not to watch them. He hadn't promised his nephew not to, either. They had made no agreement. Sanabria was more and more certain that the video had been made just before the operation. Perhaps that box contained Hugo Chávez's last words.

"You know something, Miguel," muttered Beatriz, half turning around under the covers.

Sanabria switched off the television and turned onto his side, too. They looked at each other. His wife was traveling to Panama the following day. She was going to spend time with Elisa, who was already seven months into her pregnancy.

"You must know something," Beatriz insisted, smiling. She stroked his cheek softly.

Sanabria just smiled. He gave her a kiss.

"Go to sleep. Your flight leaves pretty early in the morning."

Beatriz demurred, and wrapped herself up in the duvet.

"Just tell me he's going to die soon," she whispered.

Madeleine Butler woke up with a start. She was naked and sweating. Surrounded by shadows, she tried to figure out where she was. She wasn't in her own bed, this was not her room. She tried to find her glasses, too, but the bedside table was not where she expected it to be. There were only more shadows. She bent down slightly and let her hand graze the floor. She guessed that perhaps, before going to sleep, she had dropped her glasses on the floor. But there was nothing; she groped along the cold granite without finding a thing, any shape at all. Little by little, her shortsighted and astigmatic eyes adjusted to the darkness. It was then that she managed to make out, next to her in the bed, another two bodies, asleep, naked, as naked as she was.

If she had been dressed, if she had been wearing at least one item of clothing, perhaps it would have been easier. Madeleine ran her eyes quickly over the bed. There was not even a sock, no sign of any underwear. Next to her was a young man she vaguely recalled. He must have been around thirty, if that. Long hair that curled down his neck. He had brown skin and stubble. He wasn't snoring, but the murmur of jetties and dry sand came and went with his breathing, spreading throughout the room. He smelled of cigarettes. And rum. At the other end of the bed slept a girl who did seem familiar but whom Madeleine wasn't able to recognize then and there. Probably if she were to appear in clothes, with her hair styled, smiling, Madeleine's memory would

react straight away, she'd make some connection, would
be able to utter her name, at least. At that moment, there
was nothing. Only surprise. Impact. A naked body. Her
tangled hair across her neck; her medium-sized breasts,
like apples; her dark skin; her shaved pubis, with a single
vertical line of hair, rising up from her sex toward her
belly button. Madeleine thought about herself. About
her body. Also naked. Too pale. She wanted to move, to
quickly get out of that bed, out of the previous night that
was still this bed. She felt scared. What was she doing
there? Or worse: what had she done there? How did she
get to this point? How and why were they all in the same
place and without any clothes on? What had happened
to result, this morning, in the strange harmony of three
bodies on one mattress? Madeleine couldn't cope with
the question. She leaped out of bed and walked, stealth-
ily but rapidly, toward somewhere, looking for a bathroom. She knocked into a poster on the wall, which she
miraculously recognized in the dark as a reproduction of
a Magritte painting in which a pair of lovers with covered faces are kissing. Then she reached the bathroom
doorway. Entering, she chose not to turn on the light. She
sat down on the toilet. She urinated with relief. In there,
she remembered that the girl lying in the bed was called
Zuleyma, or actually Zuleyka. Madeleine had met so many
people in these few months. She had been in Venezuela
for almost a year now and she still wasn't sure how to
process everything she had experienced. Everything she
was experiencing, she silently corrected herself, conscious of the fact that she had just woken up next to two
naked bodies, that she was peeing in the bathroom of an
apartment she had never seen before, that she had woken
up unaware of where she had left her glasses. When she

first arrived in Caracas these images would have been impossible to hypothesize. Madeleine was much more reserved, more prudent, more timid, more demure, more proper? More moral? More respectable? The inertia of the shadows, at that time of day, nudged her toward these questions. She felt even worse. She felt like brushing her teeth, but she stayed sitting down, thinking, recalling everything that had happened since she arrived, everything that had led her to this bathroom, to this sunrise.

Erik's email had devastated her. Her boyfriend had written to her in short, crushing sentences, confirming what she had stubbornly refused to accept: yes, there was another woman, a woman who was more fun and less narrow-minded than she was; another woman who wasn't interested in Latin America and who was learning how to make sushi; another woman who hadn't become obsessed with a dictator and who was open to having anal sex. Another woman who was fun, who was happy, who had a future. Bye-bye. The written word is like a life sentence. Erik could have presented her with all of this in a conversation. It would have been a generous act, a balm. Time would have diluted or washed away his words, and sooner or later they would have been forgotten. But Erik had written them down. And Madeleine had read them. One after another. Black words, with clearly delineated shapes. With volume. With revolting exactitude. All of them freshly painted just for her. How could she forget them?

She didn't even reply. It wasn't that she didn't want to. She tried several times, but she couldn't do it. Maybe she wasn't brave enough. Perhaps she was just afraid, hugely afraid, enormously afraid, that Erik would then reply, write her another email, just the same or worse, with more short, crushing sentences. She decided to throw herself into her work, her research. And she did so with zeal. She registered as a foreign correspondent and began conducting interviews with politicians from all factions, businessmen, workers, farmers, civil servants, students, housewives, police, criminals. One day she even spoke to a group of Canadian tourists she came across at the airport. She visited working-class neighborhoods, gathered testimonies, and got excited after reading several excellent books, all written by women: *Revolution as Spectacle* by Colette Capriles, *Legacy of the Tribe* by Ana Teresa Torres, *The Sentimental Revolution* by the Spanish journalist Beatriz Lecumberri, *The Colossal State* by Margarita López Maya . . . She saw in this list a sign, sensed her own book more clearly, and it began to take shape: as time went by she grew less and less interested in writing about what was real. What was real was the least important part. What was real was always a poison, a surge of information between crossed wires. Madeleine became increasingly interested in the intangible, what was difficult to pinpoint: sensitivity, devotion and hatred, hope and fear, the intense emotions that appeared to be stirring the country. Ultimately, this was about charisma. By now she had a much better understanding of Charles Lindholm's words: "Charisma appears only in interaction with the vast majority of others who lack it." It wasn't just that Chávez had a talent, a straightforward and natural talent. It wasn't just a skill or an exceptional ability. Charisma was a relationship in which, on the whole, the nature of the leader and the extent of their power were always analyzed while very little attention was paid to the *charismafied*, to the reverent. Who were they? How did they live? What were their worries and desires? Why had they gotten so fervently hooked on this experience? Charisma was a way of life, too. A way of being with oneself and with the other. It was not a gift. It was a link.

The toilet flush handle came off in her hand.

Madeleine looked at the little aluminium object that, though she had hardly touched it, had come loose and that she was now holding between her fingers. She placed it on top of the tank and went out into the hallway. She walked along it, letting her eyes gradually adjust to the weight of the shadows. The living room was small, with wicker furniture. On the table were remains from the night before: two empty bottles of wine, one half-full bottle of wine, a bottle of rum, a couple of ashtrays, a plate with a few plantain chips left on it, several empty glasses, a single glass of water. She quickly counted the glasses to try to help her memory a little. How many people had been sitting there last night? Why couldn't she remember anything? Not even what she had drunk. She touched her genitals. Her fingers brushed against her thin strip of pubic hair, her labia, then she brought them up to her nose and breathed in deeply. What had really happened a few hours ago? Had anything happened? Could she feel anything? Could her body tell her? She walked over to a window and looked out. She could tell that she was in the Los Ruices neighborhood. In the distance, a motorbike with two riders zigzagged across Avenida Francisco de Miranda. A bit farther on, a billboard with a huge photo of the President Commander loomed. It was a remnant of the electoral campaign: "Chávez: heart of the homeland."

From the beginning, she had been warned that it wouldn't be easy, that it was, in fact, practically impossible. Chávez was a state secret. He very rarely gave personal interviews, and he would only make announcements in front of a group, whenever it suited him. At press conferences, everything was very tightly controlled and his team members wouldn't offer any information that might jeopardize them. No official seemed prepared to publicly state anything other than reiterations of the leader's speech. It was an echo chamber of almost industrial proportions. Madeleine was frustrated. It made her uneasy to be so close and yet so far. But it was thanks to this disappointment that her interest in the others began to grow, in the *charismafied*, in those who had established a special connection with the leader. Beyond the vast industry Chávez had developed to promote the cult of his personality, there had to be some reason, even if it were a vague and enigmatic motive, that could explain the bewitchment.

"Are you all right?"

The voice was soft, warm, but even so she was slightly startled. She pictured herself with no clothes on, peering out toward the balcony. Then a hand gently touched her shoulder. The voice said her name. Madeleine had no option but to turn around. There stood the young man with curly hair and stubble. He looked at her, a pleasant smile on his face. She didn't know what to say. She looked at him, naked, so comfortable, so natural. And all at once she thought of Erik. She would have liked Erik to see this image. To see her like this, standing naked before a naked stranger.

"I'm going to make coffee," he said.

He turned and moved off toward the corner where the kitchen was. She stood in silence, watching his buttocks, without knowing what to think, what to say. The first wavering rays of sunlight were starting to scratch at the windows.

It happened in April. Madeleine had traveled to the southwestern plains to visit the place where Chávez was born and to see if she could speak to someone from his family. If this didn't happen, she felt that it would still be valuable, for the context of her investigation, to get to know firsthand the place where the subject of her study was born and raised. Using those very words, she wrote an email to Professor Lindholm.

The landscape seemed oppressive to her. One endless straight line, tinged with greens and yellows, the occasional palm tree, as upright as if a bolt of lightning had landed and its tip had buried itself in the ground, trapping it there until it dried up. Animals, every now and then. Far off, close by, in the middle distance. The taxi seemed to advance by force of habit through the heat, making its way through the shimmering haze exhaled by the pavement. Always in a straight line. Madeleine had chosen to pay for many long hours in a taxi instead of taking a bus or flying. She had followed the advice of a Canadian correspondent, who had assured her it was the best option. She would have the use of the car whenever she wanted, and with the current exchange rate for black market dollars the cost was ridiculously low.

In Barinas she found lots of people who were willing to talk. Nearly everyone wanted to. With the exception of the Chávez family. She spent six hours waiting at the door to the house where she had been told Doña Elena, the president's mother, lived. In the end, she wasn't able to see her, but the woman sent her out a glass of water and a white cheese *arepa*. Madeleine visited Sabaneta, visited other nearby towns, places that supposedly had some connection with the family's history. When she had already decided to go back to Caracas she received an anonymous note, a little piece of paper with one sentence on it, scrawled by hand: *If you want to meet him, wait two more days.* That was all it said. Madeleine never found out who had sent it, but she liked to think that the improvised telegram had come from Doña Elena's house.

It was April 6, but it was also Maundy Thursday, an important date in the Catholic calendar that commemorates the crucifixion of Jesus Christ. After more rounds of radiation in Cuba, Chávez had returned to the country and had paid an unexpected visit to his parents in Barinas. Madeleine was coming out of the hotel where she was staying, by this point ready to go back to Caracas, when she almost ran into Zuleyka.

Zuleyka wasn't yet thirty and was a sound assistant who worked for one of the broadcasters assigned to the presidency. She had recorded marches, al fresco press conferences, special television programs, rallies . . . She knew the internal procedures of the televised transmissions in which the president appeared like the back of her hand. She knew what he liked and what he detested, how she should follow him with the camera, when it was necessary to do a close-up of his hands, when a humorous moment or a song would take place. Chávez was an extraordinary television producer. He never overlooked a single detail. He had managed to construct an enormously successful character and he would not allow anyone or anything to affect that success. Not even nature. Not even cancer.

Zuleyka stopped Madeleine and asked her if she was the Dutch woman.

Madeleine said nothing. She didn't understand the question. She didn't know how to respond. It was clear that the girl had confused her with another journalist.

Zuleyka was in a hurry and assumed that this brief silence, this mute doubt, was an affirmation. She and her team left all their personal luggage in the hotel and quickly got ready to leave again. Zuleyka took her by the hand and said, Let's go, we don't have much time, do you understand any Spanish or not? And then Madeleine said that she did. She was also about to say no, that she wasn't the person Zuleyka was looking for when Zuleyka told her they didn't have much time, that they were going to Mass at one of the Chávez family's properties. The president will be there. Madeleine cut her confession short and kept silent. She allowed herself to be swept along.

The experience was a revelation. She was able to experience up close the leader's infectious energy and emotion, but she was also able to get a sense of the particular details that gave his character life and potency, the difficult, perfect relationship between private and public, between melodrama and political strategy, between the feeling of truth and the reality of publicity. Madeleine stayed very close to the cameraman at all times. She could see two versions of what was happening: the real moment before her eyes, and the real moment on the monitor that was transmitting the images. It was impossible not to feel moved when faced with a crying sick man. The fragility of Chávez the human was also at the mercy of the power of Chávez the myth. Both of them used the same body.

At first it was a family service, with a few friends

and next of kin present. It was supposedly a mass to give thanks, organized by the president's own mother. Nonetheless, the most important television channels' cameras were there and, little by little, as the ceremony took place, all the other channels in the country joined in too. The public announcement was that Chávez was at a private mass. The entire audience knew that he was there for a reason, that he wasn't an extra in another show. Chávez was always the protagonist. Of course he picked up the microphone. And he spoke. In a confidential, serious tone, he spoke of himself and of Bolívar, of Don Quixote, of Che Guevara. Trembling, he raised his eyes to the sky and spoke directly to the heavens: "Christ, give me life, give me Your crown, give me Your cross, give me Your thorns, I bleed yet give me life, do not take me yet, for I still have many things to do." In his rhetorical style, so similar to that of the preachers of the electronic church, he reiterated the same idea and the same emotion in different ways. He asked for a life, even if it was painful, so as to continue fighting for the people. It was hard to tell if he was making the most ferocious, authentic confession of his life so far or just an unbeatable political broadcast. Perhaps he was doing both. Madeleine was entranced. She thought then that perhaps this was Chávez's talent, that this was one of the strengths of his appeal: everything he did seemed to have come from a detailed and rigorous script. At the same time, everything he did seemed fiercely spontaneous. People listened to him, moved and weeping. What he said was true, an emotional, irreparable truth. This relationship was charisma: this link that Chávez had reinvented. "You are Chávez": that was one of the slogans during the year's electoral campaign. He is Chávez, she is

Chávez; children are Chávez, mothers are Chávez, we are all Chávez. "Because I am no longer Chávez," he cried, stretching his voice to its limit, at one of the closing events of the campaign, "I am the people, *carajo!*"

That evening in Barinas was the closest Madeleine got to the leader in all the months she spent in Venezuela. She watched him walk past her after the ceremony. Their eyes met for two seconds. She felt herself shiver slightly. Who was this man really? How much truth and how many lies lived inside him?

Sometime later, back in the US, she saw an interview on television in which the famous presenter Larry King recalled an encounter with Chávez. He had found him charming, a really nice man. King pointed out the fact that, away from the cameras, Chávez spoke to him in perfect English, but that, when the time for the interview came, he requested the presence of an interpreter and responded to the questions in Spanish, as if he had no idea at all what the interviewer was asking him. King thought it was a strategy, that he didn't want people to know he could speak English.

Charisma is not improvised.

Madeleine spent the whole journey from Barinas back to Caracas turning this phrase over in her mind. The taxi moved forward as if not moving at all, devouring an infinite road toward a flattened horizon. And she, her head resting against the window, was thinking. They stopped at a gas station and Madeleine got out to buy water and some candy. When she got back to the car, the driver was waiting for her to pay. It was part of the agreement. Once again, she was surprised by the price of gasoline. Filling the whole tank of a car cost less than a little bottle of mineral water. That was the definition of the country. That was Venezuela. They got back in the car and set off again. They drove past abandoned towns at the side of the road, a few half-built houses with naked, barefoot children running around aimlessly. The highway was a reflection before her eyes. She felt she was slowly sinking into a thrumming, humid tunnel. She fell asleep. Or not. She wasn't sure. She was drifting in and out of sleep, swimming over a soft mist, images blending without her really knowing where they came from. She saw people she had interviewed in the working-class neighborhoods, very poor, humble people, who assured her that Chávez had changed their lives; people with difficult stories, broken families, who had always had to face acute hardships; people who, thanks to Chávez, had felt loved, important. All these faces and words merged unevenly together with what she had just experienced, with that perfect piece of melodrama, the sequence when the leader faced the gods and offered himself up as a sacrifice for the poor.

A few months later, she would return to this thought. Hope is irrational, but it can be managed. Charisma is elusive, but it is planned. But there is always an individual dimension, a sensitive sphere, that no one can control. This sphere probably also affected Chávez's relationship with himself; he, too, had grown more and more enthralled with his own radiance. It was a very difficult dynamic to handle in a healthy way. In June of 2012, during a military ceremony, Chávez declared: "Anyone who is not a Chavista is not a Venezuelan."

Vanity is the engine of history.

Madeleine fell asleep again. The taxi sped past a gigantic billboard, placed in the middle of the countryside: WE ARE ALL CHÁVEZ. In red letters.

"I don't even know your name," said Madeleine, now dressed, as she wrapped her hands around the hot cup of coffee.

"Willmer," he replied. And smiled.

Madeleine thought his smile seemed sarcastic. It hurt.

"I don't remember what happened last night," she mumbled, lowering her head, as if asking for forgiveness.

Willmer scratched his beard, looked up at the ceiling, took a sip of coffee, and finally looked at her, with the same smile.

"Nothing happened."

Madeleine felt relief beneath her tongue. She wanted, discreetly, to find out more. As they talked, she worked out that they were in Zuleyka's apartment. That, after Chávez's last rally, in the rain on Avenida Bolívar, they had all gone out dancing at a place in the city center. That Zuleyka had paid for everything. That they had drunk as if alcohol were about to go out of style. That they had carried on drinking in this apartment. That gradually people left until only the three of them remained. That Madeleine began to criticize the revolution and that Zuleyka and Willmer began to criticize Madeleine. That in the heat of the debate, who knows why but it always happens, they had started to talk about sex, too. That Willmer had said that Madeleine didn't understand the new paradigms. That he and Zuleyka were the new man and woman. That they had called her conservative and puritanical. A typical little Republican gringa. That Madeleine had said she wasn't. That Zuleyka had said she was. That Zuleyka had kissed her. That Willmer had kissed her. That one thing led to another, and another thing always leads to a bed. That Madeleine herself, trying to prove that she was not all that they said she was, had said yes, that they should go to bed together and roll around and lick and fuck each other, all three of them.

"But you fell asleep," Willmer said. "And when we went into the bedroom you were in bed, naked but snoring. Nothing happened."

Madeleine swallowed her coffee in one gulp.

"No matter how hard you try, you won't manage it. Your unconscious is bourgeois, too. You're a typical product of imperialism," Willmer said.

And he smiled again, just like before.

Sometimes, a wedding is an escape. At least it was for some of the Cubans who worked in Venezuela. One of the most practical ways to escape was to marry someone local. Faced with this, the Cuban government could do nothing. They put up obstacles, of course. They imposed tedious bureaucracy, investigations, they made everything more difficult. But, in the end, love conquered all and the comrade could leave the island to be reunited with their wife or husband. It was common practice. So much so that it was even beginning to turn into a business. There were already cases of Venezuelan men and women prepared to enter into matrimony in exchange for fair payment, a favorable cash contribution. This was not what Aylín was proposing to Fredy Lecuna. Nor was she suggesting they begin a romance. She was merely offering him a deal:

"It's simple, kiddo. I'll set you up with someone inside the CIMEQ in Havana, and, in exchange, you'll marry me. What do you think?"

Straight off, the journalist thought it sounded very complicated. He immediately thought of Tatiana and their son.

"You told me you weren't legally married."

"That's true. But even so, she's still my wife."

"I don't want to be your wife. I just want to marry you. There's a difference," she said, accentuating her voice's classic inflection.

Aylín went to the island, having secured holiday

leave, to visit her family. When she came back, in early January 2013, Fredy had his answer ready. Chávez was hidden away in Cuba and no one knew for sure how he was, what was going on with him. And what was more, the deadline for handing in his manuscript had come and gone and the status of his work was more or less the same: paralyzed. Whenever he sat down in front of the computer his fingers felt heavy, like dead vegetables.

They didn't even celebrate. It was an administrative agreement. They went to get hamburgers, shared some chips and had a few beers. Toward the end, in the second café, Fredy took longer than necessary explaining over and over again that he wasn't going to move out of his house, that he wasn't going to say anything to Tatiana or Rodrigo, that, even more importantly, neither his wife nor his son was ever to find out about this marriage, and that, if due to some circumstance or, rather, an accident, they did, then it should be made clear, sufficiently clear, that this wedding was just a contract, a strategy, a mutually beneficial link, nothing more.

And then it was Aylín's turn to agree. To all of it.

The journalist returned home feeling anxious. He felt he had guilt tattooed all over his skin, that it was impossible to hide what he had just agreed to with Aylín. He thought his wife would realize straight away, just by looking at him. He sat down in front of the computer and tried to distract himself by watching some videos he had downloaded from the internet. He had a record of how, right from the start, in 2011, Chávez had begun to develop a process of sanctifying his disease. When he came back from Cuba after the first treatment, all the country's churches and worshippers took part in public ceremonies for the sake of his health. On August 27, a traditional *bilongo* ritual was carried out, with prayers and chants; Chávez, of course, spoke of blackness and of the multicolored fatherland, gave thanks for so much love and, from a balcony of the presidential palace, declared: "Chávez will live for many more years!" A vigil was held on the 29th, to mark the beginning of the next round of chemotherapy at the Caracas military hospital. In Los Llanos, a pilgrim surfaced who said he would walk across the length of the country for the health of the head of state. At the start of September, representatives from different indigenous ethnic groups also held a religious event, a shamanic ritual. All of this would simply have been a series of separate manifestations of fervent support for a charismatic leader had the government not simultaneously implemented an enormous official media campaign that sought to establish a relationship of absolute likeness between the health of the president and the health of the nation. The whole thing was a brilliant publicity operation, with the element of melodrama managed extraordinarily well. A series of videos entitled "In the Heat of Faith" made this intention clear. Fredy Lecuna was watching one of these recordings when his wife came home with Rodrigo. The boy dashed off to his room, and Tatiana started complaining about the traffic, how irresponsible her colleagues were, how expensive the electricity bill that had just arrived was. Until she looked at her husband's face and seemed to notice something.

"What's up with you?" she asked, an enigmatic expression on her face, half surprised, half intrigued.

Fredy said that nothing was up. He lied again. It was the only thing he could think to do. The only way to survive the lie was by telling more lies. He told her he had decided to ask the publishers for another advance. He claimed, with astonishing resolve, that he had at last gotten hold of an important contact, that he couldn't say too much about it but that he was now sure that his book would be an unprecedented success, there was no doubt in his mind.

"Now's the perfect time to ask for more money."

"You think so?" asked Tatiana, fearful, hesitant. Fredy put his arms around her.

"Trust me," he said, quietly. Very quietly.

When he turned up at the publishers he was told that the general manager was expecting him. Once he had sat down in the large, empty meeting room he started to try to deal with his anxiety. He no longer felt so self-composed, and the memories of all the conversations he had had with different people at the company made him feel even more nervous. The general manager came in, smiling, settling another matter on his mobile, then giving Fredy a wave, inviting him to sit back down again, always smiling. He looked like a happy businessman.

"Now then, Lecuna," he said. "Here's how I see it: this is an industry, you signed a contract, here it is." He pointed toward a few sheets of paper on the desk.

"Yes, but . . ."

"You agreed to deliver a manuscript to us by—" He peered over at the contract, as if he couldn't quite remember. "November of last year?"

"When we spoke about it we agreed that the deadline was flexible, and that . . ." Fredy was unable to go on.

"Unfortunately, that's no longer the case," the manager interrupted. "The deadline is not so flexible, Lecuna.

Especially not the president's deadline," he added, a strange smile playing on his lips.

Fredy said nothing. He would have liked to punch him in the face, but such excesses were not in his nature. He looked down at the floor.

"Now then, Lecuna," the man repeated. "I'll be honest with you," he said, this time without smiling. "Do you know what the worst thing is about this job?" Fredy looked up, feeling obliged to look at him. "The vanity of the writers. The fucking unbelievable vanity. They're worse than TV actresses, you know. They go on and on about themselves, about what they're writing or not writing, how difficult it is to write. What they plan, wish or hope to write about. Their latest idea. Something they've just thought of. What they're attempting to write but can't, it just isn't working. . . . They all think they have less than they deserve. Do you understand what I'm saying, Lecuna?"

Lecuna understood, but said nothing. The general manager was standing up now, leaning on the desk on his fists.

"The publishing industry would be better off without writers," he concluded. "Unfortunately, that is impossible." He sat down again, looked at the contract, sighed loudly. "You have a great opportunity here. We're now in early January, Lecuna. You have two months to deliver the manuscript. If you don't do it, we'll sue you."

Surprise seized control of Fredy's face.

"And don't start with any bullshit about needing more money, will you? Come on, Lecuna," he said as he left, patting Fredy's shoulder. "Get writing!"

Fredy and Aylín got married in a simple ceremony, in a

registry office, with two witnesses they found at the last minute, and they did not celebrate afterward. Aylín did, however, wear a white dress. Simple, discreet, but white. As soon as he saw it, the journalist felt uncomfortable. The color seemed like a sentimental wink that had not been a part of the agreement. That kind of emphasis wasn't necessary.

"Shit, don't be like that. No need to be so cynical. It's not every day a girl gets married," exclaimed Aylín, her voice low, smiling.

Two hours later, Fredy Lecuna was back at home, with the news that there was an emergency, he had to leave for a trip right away, he had at last managed to pin down his contact in Cuba. He tried to talk quickly and look as if he were in a real hurry. As if the plane were waiting for him out in the street, opposite the apartment building. He stressed how important his discovery was, that there was a man prepared to talk to him in Havana, it was the twist he had been looking for, the revelation he so desperately needed to finish his book.

"What do you think Hemingway did? Stayed at home waiting for the story to come knocking at his door?" Fredy said, flinging clothes rapidly into a small suitcase.

"You are not Hemingway, Fredy. Don't bullshit me," said his wife, quite sensibly.

And then there was nothing for it but to confess that he had failed at the publishers. He told her about the meeting with the general manager, about the ultimatum he'd been given, the threat of legal action. She spoke about Andreína Mijares, her constant pressure, the stress of living this way, with the fear that at any moment they could end up homeless. He stubbornly repeated the story of his supposed contact in Havana, a hypothetical nurse or paramedic who worked for the CIMEQ, the exclusive hospital where Chávez was being treated. She once again called into question how Fredy had handled the book project, his countless lost days, his mysteries and his secrets, the relationship with that Cuban woman who worked for the government, his lack of productivity for so many months. The promise of the contact on the island didn't inspire any confidence in her.

"It's a unique opportunity," he said.

"It might all be a big lie," she pointed out.

He said that it wasn't, and she said that it was. There is nothing more destructive than insecurity. And Tatiana had plenty of it, she had already built up far too much. Fredy tied himself up in knots trying to pretend, to act natural. Just the idea of Tatiana finding out he had gotten married to Aylín was enough to make him tremble. Tatiana said:

"It might be a trick, a scam! You don't even know if this woman is lying to you, if this contact even exists! You don't even know her name!"

And Fredy started talking about Hemingway again.

In the end, the volume rose and rose and the words flew through the air, as if trying to escape from hot oil.

"What if Andreína Mijares turns up with a court order and throws us out?" asked Tatiana.

"That's not possible!" exclaimed Fredy.

"That's what you say," she replied, adding, "but what if it does happen?"

Fredy paced around impatiently, waving his hands in the air, before finally turning to face her.

"What if armed robbers break in right now and shoot us dead? Eh? Or I have a heart attack suddenly and die? Or my plane crashes tonight?"

They both fell silent for a moment. Their gaze locked in an enraged impasse. It was a silent spark, a mute shock. There are few things more unifying than shared rage.

"You know what?" Tatiana whispered. "Don't ask me why, but sometimes I feel like you won't come back."

Fredy sensed a tremor from within, a small convulsion stretching out its folds, unleashing increasingly broad movements. He made an effort and contained himself, disguised his feelings once again, looked lovingly at his wife and sighed as he said, "What are you talking about, my love? How can you say that?"

And he embraced her. Kissed her. Tatiana stood her ground, calmly devastated.

During the entire flight to Havana, his brow remained furrowed, his gaze lost in the distance. Aylín even thought he was afraid of flying. The third time they hit turbulence, she took his hand. The journalist gently pulled it free and remained silent. Then Aylín said that they had to have a serious talk. She explained that they would need to put on a little bit of an act on the island. It wasn't a question of romance, it was strictly about security. Suspicion of the other was part of the system of control in Cuba. It was a system based on mutual vigilance.

"We can't take any chances," she told him.

Essentially, Aylín wanted him to pretend a little.

"You can't go around with that look on your face when you're with me," she said. "People will get suspicious; do you know what I mean?"

All she was asking was for him to act more or less genuine. Like he was genuinely happy, genuinely joyful—just a little genuine love.

"As if we really were newlyweds, for God's sake."

As the plane descended, and the destination became more land and less sea, Fredy Lecuna began thinking about the path that was leading him toward that island, to that moment when, suddenly, cheesy sentimentality had become a kind of journalism.

Aylín's entire family was waiting for them at the airport.

"Smile, honey. Give me a kiss."

"A journalist?" the official asked, his guard immediately up.

Andreína Mijares explained that her tenant was unemployed. He was a journalist without a job. This fact seemed to reassure the official. He then said something about the way the right manipulated the media and quoted one of President Commander Hugo Chávez's phrases.

Andreína didn't say a word. But she made a face that suggested she agreed. Or at least she thought she did. It was an expression squeezed out from within her bones, a strained deception. She still couldn't believe she was sitting there, chatting with the enemy.

Two days earlier, Carolina Troconis had called her up and told her she had found a way to solve her problem. All she gave her was a telephone number and a forewarning:

"They're Chavistas," she said. "Be prepared!"

Andreína Mijares went to a local government office for a meeting with an official. He looked like a normal man to her, a classic bureaucrat, with the face of someone who had swallowed a procedures manual. She told him everything, in great detail, showing him several documents. He listened patiently and respectfully, and then moved the pile of papers she had brought to one side and explained that the situation would have to be resolved in another way. Andreína Mijares didn't understand, or wasn't certain that she understood what she thought she was understanding. She thought the man was asking her for money. The civil servant smiled and explained that he just wanted to help her, that he was just trying to save her from having to go through soul-destroying paperwork. Andreína still didn't understand.

"You'll have to break in."

Andreína's face: bewilderment, a cognitive glitch.

"None of this will work," said the civil servant, referring to the paperwork.

"So? What can I do?"

"The only way out of this is for you to enter by force, ma'am. You'll have to break into your own house."

Two days later, Andreína Mijares found herself in the middle of Petare, the vast mountain slopes covered in slums in east Caracas. Never in her life had she set foot in this place. Poverty, to her, was a faraway country, the distant murmur of statistics. She didn't really know who the poor were, either. What did this word really mean? What were they like? What did they feel, what did they think? Standing outside one of the entrances to the neighborhood of San Blas, she couldn't stop asking herself these questions. Without realizing it, she had her arms crossed in front of her chest, gripping her handbag. She was waiting, just as she had been told to do. In the exact spot. Standing on the sidewalk. A little off to the right, pulled over, was the taxi she had hired specially to take her here, wait for her, and take her back to the city again. Back to what she believed was the city. Or, at least, *her* city. It was eight in the morning and many people were walking past, going up or down the road. They were also walking up and down various flights of steps that sliced through the areas filled with houses. This was a working-class neighborhood, she told herself. All these people were the poor, she thought. Perhaps she only saw naive stereotypes. Prejudices. And fear. A lot of fear. They looked at her, too. Some directly, others out of the corners of their eyes; some quickly, hurriedly, others with more curiosity. But they could see she was out of place. That she wasn't one of them. That she was a foreigner in the kingdom of the poor.

"It's like another country, isn't it?"

Andreína didn't flinch, didn't move, didn't know how to react. She felt the presence behind her take slow steps around her, gradually emerging, until the woman with that voice and a half-smile was in front of her.

"Don't you think? This place is pretty different from where you live, isn't it?"

After explaining how the only chance she had of getting her house back was if she became a squatter in it, the official had spent quite some time describing the arduous path of the revolution. He said things like: It's not easy building socialism upon the foundations of a rentier state. Or: We are a revolution in progress, in transition, we still haven't overcome the vices of the past, the legacy of capitalism. And also: It's impossible to substitute one model for another overnight. We are taking a hybrid route.

"I hope that makes sense," he concluded, looking at her, as if wrapping up a teacher-training workshop. "I'm not sure if you see where I'm coming from," he added.

Andreína was still open-mouthed, astonished. She was struggling to comprehend the proposal. She could not even imagine it.

"I'd be more than happy," the civil servant said insistently, "to put you in touch with the relevant people. They are," he assured her, "very experienced colleagues."

He was referring to three women, two of them linked to the party, who had already participated in several occupations, overseeing various people in some of the working-class invasions that had been reported in the city in the past few years.

"They're not amateurs. They can help you with your house."

And he went on explaining that, naturally, Andreína would have to pay the three women's fees, which obviously wasn't a contribution to the party, that certainly wasn't the case, but rather a payment for a job done, the women had to be compensated for the task or labor they would undertake. Andreína remained dumbstruck, but she agreed to everything. The civil servant made a telephone call and then wrote an address down on a piece of paper.

"Do you by any chance know the neighborhood of San Blas de Petare, ma'am?" he asked.

Their names: Virginia, Mildred, and Dusty. (Or, at least, "Dusty" was what the first two called the third.) Virginia looked around forty. She was the oldest. She was also the fattest. But she didn't seem to care much. She was wearing a pair of tight blue Lycra leggings that reached her waist and a sleeveless top, narrow and slight, that barely covered her breasts, leaving a round, generous belly exposed. At first glance she seemed to be the leader of the three. Mildred was slender, bony. Andreína guessed she was around thirty-five. She also thought she had indigenous features. She imagined she might be a peasant, or part-peasant—that she had a relatively recent rural past. Mildred didn't speak much but had a different way of looking at her surroundings. As if she were always seeing everything twice. Dusty was the youngest, perhaps under thirty. She had three earrings in her left ear and a tattoo on her left hand. She was chewing gum and wearing an olive-green beret. All three women were dark-skinned. Why did she think of the word "dark-skinned"? Why not "black"? Were they dark-skinned or black? What was the difference? She felt nervous, for no reason. Was it more polite to say dark-skinned than to say black? Was it more or less aggressive? Was saying black aggressive? Was it more polite, fair, appropriate? Was this the reason the government had issued a decree calling for people to be vigilant about language, promoting the public use of the term "of African descent"? They're three lovely black girls, the government official had said. Don't you worry, Ma'am. You'll get on very well. They were right there in front of her at that very moment and she felt only awkward, flustered, out of place.

"You're nervous."

"Yes, a bit."

"When I found her she was as white as a sheet. She's a little posh girl who's come to the slums for the first time. That's what's the matter."

"Nothing's going to happen to you while you're with us," the fat one said, looking directly at her. "Tell us what the problem is."

Andreína told them. Her story was constantly interrupted. One of the women would comment on something and this would trigger a brief conversation among the three of them. They spoke boldly, as if Andreína weren't there—recounting some anecdote, laughing raucously, joking, trying to make sense of Andreína's story, until Virginia wondered whether it was time to get back to the story and, with a movement of her hand, gave Andreína the floor again. Once she had finished, the three women looked at each other and exchanged knowing looks. Virginia looked directly at her again and said simply:

"Done."

They didn't burden her with more details. One of them said: "Don't worry." Another said: "We'll take care of it." Dusty added: "It'll be easy." And they told her they would call her in two or three weeks to give her the date and price. As simple as that. But Andreína wanted to know more. She was bursting with questions. How would they proceed? They'd enter the apartment and— then what? What would happen next? What would they do once they were inside? What would be the modus operandi then? Would there be any kind of violence at all? She was troubled by the thought that she might be organizing something hostile or illegal. She was worried she couldn't control what might happen. The presence of a minor in the apartment frightened her, the risks that came with it.

"The boy's a fucking gift. Don't worry about him," Dusty exclaimed. "It helps that he's there."

Mildred said only: "Uh-huh."

And Virginia:

"Don't get worked up. We'll use him to make this woman get out of your house more quickly. That's what you want, isn't it?"

Rodrigo put on his headphones. The door to his room was closed and he was sitting at his computer, chatting online. He had made a bet with his school friends. He was the only one who believed that Butterfly could be a girl his age. Sergio said she was old, like thirty, with a mustache and a wart on one of her boobs. Franklin said she must be a faggot like Henry Cárdenas, the camp kid from the other group. Rodrigo, his ego bruised, had said that Butterfly was real, that they were going out, that they were in a relationship. The other boys laughed, teasing him. That's how the bet was born, and this was why Rodrigo was typing with urgent fingertips.

I want to see you.

What for?

To see you.

Silence. Pause. Emptiness.

To see what you look like, he insisted.

And again, silence, and pause, and more emptiness.

You already know what I look like. I have to go. My mum's calling me.

She had decided to lie. Not just to Vampire. To the rest of the world, too. She wasn't sure how long this fictitious life could go on, but it was the best way to keep herself alive. Only a month had gone by. Up until now, she had managed to deflect a telephone call from an aunt and another from Cecilia, her godmother. Luckily, they were both in San Cristóbal. She told both of them the same thing. Her mother was ill, had lost her voice, the doctor had forbidden her to smoke or speak. María was looking after her. Cecilia said she would come to Caracas soon. Her aunt sent her best wishes and recommended her mother drink water boiled with a red onion, three star anises, and a few drops of rum.

María began repeating her mother's routines. One habit: bathe at six in the evening and use two towels to dry herself. Her mother performed this ritual every day with mechanical precision. María would know it was six o'clock because she could hear the sound of the shower, the drops falling and hitting the grey tiles. She would usually spend ten minutes beneath the water and then dry herself, using one towel for her body and another for her hair. María started doing the same, even though she didn't have enough body or hair for it, even though there was always an excess of fabric. She would come out of the bathroom with one towel dragging on the floor, trying to keep the other one balanced on top of her head. Then, naked, she would look at herself in the mirror hanging on the back of the door of her mother's room. That slender, still-shapeless body didn't look much like her mother's. Sometimes she would touch her chest and ask herself what it would be like to have breasts. What it will be like. And she would keep looking. Then she would imagine herself with breasts, and taller, and then she would see her mother too, outlined in the mirror, smiling at her.

Another habit: applying cream to her face before going to sleep. María remembered that, every night, her mother would sit on the bed, take a plastic pot, and gently cover her face with the near-white cream. María recalled one night in particular: she was barefoot and in pajamas, her legs crossed, sitting on the bed next to her mother, looking at her. Her mother talked to her about skin, told her this helped prevent it from drying out. María said that it smelled gross and her mother smiled and said that she would have to use it one day, and then she would remember her. And she put a little blob of cream on the tip of María's nose. They both laughed. María found the tub with the cream on a shelf in the bathroom. She had to use a chair from the dining room to reach it. But she was determined. From that day onward, every night, before going to bed, she sat on the bed and spread the near-white cream all over her face.

In the living room, the television continued talking to itself. Always. From six in the morning until ten at night. Just like before.

The chasm left behind by the death of another can only be obscured by the fear of one's own death. María was very young, was not yet old enough to imagine her own death that seriously. After mourning, after days spent paralyzed on her mother's bed, clinging to the bedclothes and the urge to cry, she suddenly started to retrieve the everyday rituals, the domestic procedures they had had before; she reestablished the same ceremonies that had defined their existence, as if her mother were still alive. In a cupboard drawer she found three new checkbooks inside a plastic bag. It proved easy for her to fake her mother's signature. Her first trip was to the little grocery store on the ground floor of the building on the corner. She knew the owner, an old Portuguese man from Madeira, who chewed his Spanish words in a charming way. Ever since they had stopped going to the local supermarket they would stock up here every week. María made her first purchase and her first deal on this one and only visit. She was very nervous. She felt like her voice was shaking. She told the Portuguese man that she needed to talk to him, that it was a personal matter. Puzzled, not a little disconcerted, the man took her into the back of the shop, where there were crates of tomatoes stacked up on top of each other. María told him that her mother was ill, that the doctor had ordered her to rest, that she couldn't get out of bed, that she couldn't even speak.

"What's wrong with her?" asked the Portuguese man, surprised.

"I don't really know," said María, looking down at the floor. "I think it's got something to do with her smoking," she added.

The Portuguese man imagined the worst and offered himself up for whatever she needed. He seemed to be totally willing for María to call up from now on and order her shopping by telephone. One of his employees would deliver everything up to her apartment and she would pay by check. Thank you very much, she said, still feeling the heat of the lie in her cheeks. The Portuguese man said that she was welcome, sent his regards to her mother and, by way of a goodbye, ruffled her hair a little clumsily. He seemed genuinely distressed.

In her mother's telephone book, on the last page, she found the telephone password of her bank account. Using the internet, she made sure all the bills would be paid by direct debit. She took up her studies again with almost the same discipline she had before. She successfully resolved a few domestic dramas, including killing a cockroach in the kitchen. She spent several hours in front of the mirror with a pair of scissors in one hand and a fashion magazine in the other, building up the courage to cut her own hair. She bravely approached her mother's long work table. The eyes, the scissors, the tweezers. The empty chair. Sometimes, at the end of the afternoon, she would sit on the table to look out the window. It was the only place from which she could see the street. Astonished, bewildered. As if she were watching a film. As if she were watching people walking through snow.

One afternoon, a light bulb blew. She was eating spaghetti with tuna, one of her mother's favorite recipes. It was simple: garlic and onion with a bit of oil in a frying pan, over a low heat. Then you added a can of tuna. A spoonful of tomato purée and some water. You mixed it and let it cook for a while, always at a low heat. The light bulb exploded in the kitchen. The little shards of glass flew everywhere. Some fell into the frying pan, into what remained of the sauce. The explosion left her paralyzed. Cautiously, she approached the kitchen. She stuck her head in first, looked around, didn't understand what could have happened. Only when she went in and heard the crunch of fine glass beneath her sandals did she look up. Changing the bulb was a real feat. She wouldn't have managed it without Vampire's help.

My mum can't get out of bed. I've got to change it myself.

Do you have a stepladder?

No. But I've got a stool.

Is it really high up?

It's on the ceiling.

That doesn't mean anything. Your ceiling might be a low one.

I don't know. Let me check.

They always chatted at night. In this way, too, María continued to act as if, in some secret way, her mother was still there, keeping an eye on her. They were her rules.

That was what had survived. A system governed by fear of the outside world, a system of education and control. The life they had shared.

It looks high to me. But I could use the stool to get up onto the counter and from there I could reach it.

And do you have the new bulb?

I found two in the cupboard. I'll see if they fit.

I could come and help you if you want.

The phrase flickered for a few seconds on the computer screen's gleaming surface. María felt a piercing chill in her throat. Her knees were shaking, too. She opened her mouth in astonishment. She closed it, as if trying to stop the shock from leaving her. This was Vampire's first move. A signal sent into no-man's-land. Like a flare soaring across the sky. María moved away from the computer as if it might burn her. Without taking her eyes off it, she took two steps back and leaned against the edge of her bed.

Are you still there?

Have you left?

Over the next few days, the tension kept growing, always in the same direction, toward the same destination. After two or three sentences, or sometimes after five or six, or ten or twelve, Vampire would corner María. He wanted more. He wanted to know more. Being boyfriend and girlfriend couldn't just be this interaction, stuck in the same position. Vampire felt that their online chat was a parking lot, an enclosed space where they would end up parking and exchanging a few words. He liked chatting with her, but what we like can become tired, it fades, it needs to be renewed. Desire is movement. One Sunday he gave her an ultimatum: either we meet up or we stop being boyfriend and girlfriend. María was upset. She logged off without a word. She was probably more rattled and nervous than she was angry.

They went a week and a half without speaking, but, little by little, her resolve weakened. Every night, looking through the dark at the switched-off computer screen, María softened. Until one night she returned to the chat room. She stayed visible for a while. Vampire was visible, too. His avatar hadn't changed. But neither of them made the first move. They were floating among multiple conversations, looking at each other but not daring to act. An hour and a half later, Vampire disappeared. María felt desolate. What had at first been indignation was quickly replaced by anxiety: was this how it would be from now on? Had they broken up? Had they broken up forever? Would she never chat with Vampire again? Were they not even friends anymore? The following night, she entered the chat room even earlier, and anxiously waited for him. She only left the computer for a few short seconds, when she had to go to the bathroom to wipe her hands dry. Why were they sweating? What was this? What was happening? When at last Vampire's icon appeared like a little flash inside the screen, María pounced:

Are you angry with me?

There was no reply. In a chat room silence can mean so many things.

You don't talk to me anymore.

You're the one who's not talking to me.

I'm talking to you now.

And I'm answering you.

They went on like this until they grew tired, until

María accepted defeat, clasped her hands together. She wanted to bite her nails, her fingers. She pressed her legs together, too. She felt a giddiness below her belly button and wrote and said she agreed and that yes, they should see each other.

Do you have a camera?

He said goodbye to Beatriz at the airport and an hour and a half later he was back at home. It was six in the evening on February 20. Elisa was going to give birth in March, Beatriz had planned to get there a month beforehand to help her and keep her company. Sanabria had decided to stay behind. Two months in Panama seemed to him like an eternity.

As soon as he got home, he poured himself a whiskey. He took the box from the study and put it on the low table in the living room, then sat down on the sofa, in front of the television. He waited a few minutes until the warmth of the alcohol softened the hard edges of the ice. He stared distractedly at the lifeless television screen in the dim light. He wondered how much of the country's recent history had taken place on the television. Was it even possible to separate history from the television? he asked himself. All you had to do was press a button to switch reality, or what some people believed to be reality, on or off.

He put his glass down on the table and picked up the small wooden chest. The cigar box had become a troubling presence in his house. Every day he moved it to a different place, always within the study, but he needed to move it, to touch it, to carry it from one bookshelf to another. Sometimes he even felt the urgent need to pick it up several times in the same day, to feel its hard edges between his fingers, to put it somewhere else. It was as if this small wooden container was alive, vaguely and somehow elusively alive, in a way that left no trace—not conspicuous but certainly palpable. Indecipherably, dangerously alive.

He hesitated for a few seconds and then, with his left hand, took out the mobile. He switched it on. Slowly the little screen lit up. Sanabria's fingers moved quickly, he opened the telephone's menu and found two videos. Both were labeled with the same letters: Ch1 and Ch2. He wavered again for a moment. Was he doing the right thing?

Didn't this feel a bit indecent, a bit morbid? Knowledge was a powerful charm. Perhaps, after watching those videos, nothing would be the same again. Throughout the past weeks he had felt that the box was breathing but, at that moment, with the telephone in his hand, he felt something else, a peculiar heat, a nearby dread, the feeling of stepping off a precipice. Did he really want to see these images?

Chávez's absence was causing more and more unease—above all, because there were no direct messages from the president. Everything people knew about him came from other people, a few officials, like the government's high command, or people who weren't officials, such as journalists or mere spectators who claimed to have clandestine sources. Speculation had continued to reign and, as the days went by, it seemed to seize the country completely. The truth was an increasingly fragile experience. There was no longer any pretense: Chávez's health was not a medical but a religious matter. The government's high command began speaking like priests. The state began to look like a church.

However much the government insisted on denying

it, the whole process was strange. The feigned air of normality sharply contrasted with feelings of confusion, mixed up with everyday tension. The official bulletins, read out by the minister of communication, mixed vague medical information with accusations of psychological warfare and government propaganda. They all ended, invariably, with the cry "Viva Chávez!," which occasionally felt less like a celebratory affirmation and more like a rhetoric of absence, a way of preparing for the final farewell.

In just a few weeks, the country had experienced a dizzying process, full of intrigue and suspense. On December 11 the president underwent surgery in Havana, and the next day it was reported that the intervention had been "complex, difficult and delicate" and that, therefore, "the post-surgery process" would also be "complex and difficult." On December 14 an announcement was made that the leader was in recovery. Four days later it was mentioned for the first time that he was suffering from a "respiratory infection." On Christmas Eve, the public was informed that Chávez "was walking, doing exercises," and that he wished the whole country a very merry Christmas. On December 28, the vice president read out a message from Chávez to the national Bolivarian armed forces. He assured them that Chávez himself had written the soldiers' end-of-year greeting. "There is a revolution underway here," declared the missive. On December 30, it was announced that the patient had improved, but only a little, that he remained in a "delicate" state, "not without complications." On December 31, the government organized a ceremony in honor and support of the president in the Plaza Bolívar in Caracas. It was called "Now More Than Ever, With Chávez."

They guaranteed that, from Havana, Chávez was watching the event on television. On January 1, 2013, one of the government ministers tweeted from Cuba asking Venezuelans not to believe the "malicious rumors" about the president's health. Two days later officials informed the public that the president was suffering from a "severe pulmonary infection." Four days later it was said that the situation was "unchanging." Chávez was not able, as was expected and as was laid out in the constitution, to be sworn in for his next term as the country's president. On January 10 a "symbolic swearing-in ceremony" was carried out in the president's residence, the Palacio de Miraflores. The ceremony was attended by the presidents of Uruguay, Bolivia, and Nicaragua and was hosted by a well-known and shrill presenter from Venezuelan television. On January 13, after a meeting attended by the government's political team in Cuba, it was reported that the patient's physical state remained delicate but that his "medical progress" was positive. Ten days later, with no more information other than the same routine headlines, a Spanish newspaper published a photograph supposedly showing Chávez intubated and in an intensive care unit. The photograph was fake and the article itself was terrible. The journalist apologized. On January 26 it was announced that Chávez had overcome his respiratory failure. On January 29, via a message on social media, it was reported that Chávez was "in full command of his mental faculties" and "giving orders like never before." On February 6 Fidel Castro himself stated that "Chávez is much better, he's recovering." On February 10, the governing party carried out a large-scale activity that involved placing mailboxes in every municipality of the country so that people could send the president letters of love and support. Five days later photographs appeared showing the leader reading the Cuban state newspaper *Granma* with his daughters. The public was informed that Chávez was using a tracheal tube, which helped him to breathe but meant he could not speak. However, none of this, it was said, prevented the president from remaining "conscious and focused on governing." Three days later, in the early hours of February 18, Chávez returned to Caracas to continue his treatment. No one saw him disembark from the plane. No one saw him enter the military hospital. No one saw him. The only thing anyone could see was a single message posted on his social media account. Never before had he been so quiet for so long. He was no longer himself. His overwhelming presence, his absolute prominence, no longer existed. He was merely something that was referred to now. A feeble echo, growing ever fainter. A silence.

Perhaps Sanabria's premonition had come true. Perhaps Chávez's last words were there, inside a box. Locked away in a cheap telephone. But still beating.

Vladimir had disappeared weeks ago. Sanabria had tried to contact him by every means possible but he hadn't succeeded. Ever since Vladimir had come back from Havana in December, when he turned up at his uncle's house asking him to hide this box, Sanabria had gradually heard less from his nephew. He asked himself more than once why Vladimir had entrusted him with the box. Why had he chosen his uncle? Did he perhaps know or had he guessed what might be in those videos? What about his instructions to hand them over to a foreign journalist? What did that mean? Why could nothing in this country ever be normal, natural? Why did everything always have to seem like a plot, a conspiracy?

For a moment, Sanabria thought that Chávez would certainly never have dreamed of an ending like this. It was the worst of all his possible endings. Watching history in the making from the sidelines of his incurable illness. Unable to speak. Unable to say a word. Punished. Moving his tongue around inside his mouth. And nothing else. His tongue going in circles, like a lizard, trapped. And nothing else. Just thirst. So thirsty.

He watched the two videos. Several times. Slowly, trying to focus on the details. Then he put the phone back in the box and, soon afterward, put the box on the third shelf in the study, on the right-hand side of the television. He poured himself a third whiskey and sat down on a stool in the kitchen. He didn't pick up a mandarin, but he did listen to the faraway sound of cars flying past on the highway.

When the telephone rang, he supposed it was his wife, settled in by now at their daughter's house in Panama. He didn't move. He didn't want to talk to anybody. He stayed by the window, allowing himself to drift along in the whiskey's gentle buzz, softly and slowly. He let the telephone ring, the sound reverberating, until the answering machine came on. It was then that he heard a strange voice with a curious Spanish accent.

"Good evening. My name is Madeleine Butler."

"How good is your Spanish? OK. Let me know if I'm talking too fast, then. Stop me whenever you like.

"I've always been poor. And when I say always, I mean always: an always that includes my parents and my parents' parents and my parents' parents' parents and on and on until infinity, all of them poor, totally fucked. We thought that being poor was forever, that it was just something in our nature, you know. We used to think things like that without realizing, reciting them more than actually thinking them, believing it was what we really thought. I don't know if that makes sense. When you're fucked you can't think straight. Everything's borrowed. Even ideas. And you walk through life with nothing. Or with just your bones, your skin, which is basically nothing too, because it's the only thing that's free in this world: what we're born with, what we have on when we first open our eyes and look around terrified, as if we're thinking, 'So this is life?'

"I'm the fifth child of seven. All from the same mother, that's what connects us. Gloria, the eldest, is the daughter of a guy Mum always refused to speak about. We thought he was a boyfriend she had in Caripe, before she moved to Caracas. Then come Luis, Trina, and Robinson. They're all Pedro's kids. He lived with my mum for years. But he drank a lot. He was a musician and hit the bottle pretty hard. My mum ended up kicking him out of the house and spent two years on her own. Until she met my dad. My dad was called Bruno and he was Colombian, from

151

the coast. He lived in Acarigua with a woman and two
children. Do you know Acarigua? Have you been there?
No, no, it's in the midwest, kind of toward the plains if
you're coming from Barquisimeto. But it doesn't matter,
anyway. The thing is, Bruno had a sister who lived in the
neighborhood, in Caracas. She was our neighbor and
her name was Marciana. I remember it well because we
found it really funny. It seemed like a joke. How could
someone be named after a Martian? Apparently it's common in Colombia. At least, that's what she told us. The
point is that, one day, Bruno came to visit Marciana and
as soon as he saw my mum he became completely tongue-
tied. Time froze. He couldn't move. Mum was young, she
would have been around thirty-something and she was
really beautiful and good fun. They got together soon
after that and Bruno came to stay, for longer and longer, and then he started moving in, little by little, until he
stopped going back to Acarigua at all. He sent a friend
to get his things one day and that was it. He moved in
with us. I say 'us' even though I hadn't been born yet, but
I was about to be. I was Bruno and my mum's first. After
me came Yocelin and then Yulman. My dad looked after
all of us, to the point that my older siblings called him
Dad, too. Only Gloria called him by his name, but she
was seven years old by the time he came into our house.
Yes, he died, that's right. Three years ago. It was really
shitty luck.

"One night he got some stomach thing, it began with
a stabbing pain, he thought he'd eaten something that
hadn't gone down well, he thought it was nothing but it
turned out to be really serious, they even say it could have
been a hemorrhage. Yocelin, who lives with her husband
in my mum's house, grabbed him, loaded him into the

car and sped off. But A&E at the Pérez de León Hospital was closed. They didn't want to admit him because they didn't have any surgical equipment. A nurse told us they didn't even have alcohol. So they had to go to Domingo Luciani Hospital, nearby, in El Llanito. Again, no luck. A&E there had been taken over by a gang. Seems there was a fight between two gangs. Some thug had been shot full of holes and his people had come to the hospital and taken over A&E. The whole place was full of guys with guns. They said that there were guys with crowbars even inside the operating theater, making sure all the bullets were fished out of their guy. And outside too, in the corridors, there were people from the same gang, all of them armed. They were on the lookout. They thought that the other gang might jump them right there. There was one doctor crying, kind of hysterical, shouting out, calling for help. The police? No way. They'd have to be idiots. They don't get involved in that kind of thing. It's one thing to be a policeman and another to be suicidal.

"This is what we like to call playing roulette. Like a roulette wheel, you know? You go from one place to another and you never get anywhere. You spend your whole life just going around in circles. And that's what happened. And the old man died on us in the car. On the way from Domingo Luciani Hospital to the Universidad Central Clinical Hospital. He never got there. At some point along the way, he stayed where he was. Yocelin says he was gasping for breath, spitting out loads of blood. Mum was in the front seat, next to Eduardo, who's Yocelin's husband and who makes out like he's a tough guy but that night he was really scared, he didn't want a dead guy in his car. But that's what happened. And Yocelin had a really hard time. The old man died on her lap. She still hasn't gotten over it. All she remembers, the story she tells, is that she was looking at him and, all of a sudden, his eyes went all small. And his lips were white. And he said, don't let me die, please. And that was it. It was over. That was the last thing he said. Nearly all of us were there at the Universidad Central, waiting for them. It was an awful moment. The car arrived and there was no life left. Yocelin was just crying in the back seat. And my mum couldn't even move. It was awful. We were all in a bad way. It was a shitty night. That was the first time we argued about Chávez.

"There have never been any squalids in my family. Not one. Not even Gloria, who's the most stuck-up, the one who thinks she's different. She works in a bank. She's assistant manager at a branch out east. The people there have pretty much brainwashed her. But even so, she's not a squalid. She doesn't like the government, fine; but she doesn't like the opposition, either. That night? Oh yeah, of course. The thing is we were all nervous, we all felt that pain you get right there, stuck in your throat. My mum was crying, all of us were crying. And we were all think-ing the same thing: the motherfucking hospitals in this country, *el coño de su madre*. You know what that means, don't you? You know what *el coño de su madre* means? Because that's a very Venezuelan phrase, it's something we say all the time. That's why I was asking. Uh-huh. That's right. Where was I? Oh yeah, exactly. That's what we were doing. Motherfucking hospitals. Motherfucking health. Motherfucking everything. Until Yulman said it: Motherfucking Chávez. And that pissed me off and I told him not to bring Chávez into this, it wasn't his fault. And we all started talking, shouting, fighting. That had never happened to us before. But now I realize that it wasn't really a political argument. It was just a way of getting some of the pain out of our system, you know?

"Maybe it's hard for you to understand, maybe you don't get it. People used to look down on us here. For being poor, for being the way we are. You could feel it out in the street, even, in the way people looked at us. We lived up on the hill, high up, and the city was down below. The city belonged to them. Like it was their house. And we were a different kind of people. Outsiders, different, bad, dangerous. Poor. You can feel it on your skin, in people's looks, it's like something invisible but very powerful that you can really feel. But if you aren't poor, you have no idea. You can go around thinking everything's normal. That life's just like that. That's it.

"I have a memory from when I was a little girl. My dad was working as a builder. Sometimes he'd be working on a building or some construction job. And sometimes he would moonlight, do little jobs on the side, piecework, in family homes. One Saturday he said to me: Do you want to see a family home? Do you want to see how people live? I must have been around six or seven years old. And just listen to the way I'm telling you the story, the words I'm using. Because that's how my dad said it to me. 'Family home,' 'people.' As if our house, the house we all lived in, in our neighborhood, was something else, as if it wasn't a house and we weren't a family. As if we weren't people, or not as much as they were. I don't know if that makes sense.

"That Saturday he took me with him. We went down into the city together. My mum put me in a green dress that I really liked and put little bows in my hair, in bunches. And off we went. It took about an hour and a half to get there. And from where we got off the bus, we

had to walk for ages. It was a housing development full of
huge houses, with gardens, some with pools. My dad was
going to plaster one of the walls in the patio. I remember the two of us there, him loading the trowel up with
cement, and me sitting quietly, looking at everything, so
surprised. The sun was strong that day, we were really
hot. And I said, Dad, I'm thirsty. And he told me to go
into the kitchen and ask Señora Carmen for some water.
Señora Carmen worked in the house. She was like us,
but she was wearing a pale-blue uniform. When I went
in, the woman who owned the house was in the kitchen,
too. She was a tall, white lady, I thought she looked ele-
gant. I don't know. But I asked for my water and Señora
Carmen picked up a glass and went over to the fridge
to pour me some water, but, here's the good part, the
owner of the house said no, not in that glass. 'Those are
our glasses,' she said. I looked at the glass and it was just
a glass, quite normal, there was nothing special about it.
The owner of the house opened a cupboard and took out
a plastic cup and gave it to Señora Carmen. Give her this
one, she said. And she smiled at me. She said something
else I can't remember and went off somewhere. It may
seem silly, but it stayed with me. It probably seems like
nothing to you, just a dumb thing, what do I know. But
it was a big deal for me. I don't know. I felt like I was different. Different but bad. That I couldn't use her things.
That I couldn't drink water in the same glasses they
used. That I was so different that I might make them
dirty, stain them.

"That's why I'm telling you that Chávez changed my
life. Because he's like us, and he really stood up to all those
people. He changed my life, but up here, in my mind. He
changed my way of thinking, of seeing, of seeing myself.

What's he given me? Specifically, you mean? How can I put this? You see, we had nothing, we were nobodies; or more like: we felt like nobodies, that we weren't worth anything, that we didn't matter. And that's what changed with Chávez. That's what he gave us. Maybe you can't get it. You're a gringa, and you're white. It's completely different. You have to have lived it. Like I said before, it's about your skin, your heart. Basically, I love him because he's ugly and poor, like me. And look where he is, look how far he got. He's the only one who's spoken up for us. I don't know if that makes sense. Chávez taught me to be me and not to be ashamed. Do you understand?"

"On an island, the only thing that matters, really, is who's arriving and who's leaving. That's the only news."

The man spoke with confidence, as if his words were worth repeating. He was wearing a pair of shorts and a vest. It was Omar, Aylín's brother. He'd made a real effort to become a sort of personal tutor to Fredy. He wanted to be his private guide to Havana and what it meant to be Cuban. He knew everything, he always had a supposedly clever explanation ready, a surprising story, an irrefutable argument. After three days, the journalist had come to realize that any attempt to shut him up was useless. It was far more effective, in the long term, to feign interest and look directly at him, then wait until his voice began to resemble the distant, hoarse murmur of the breakwater.

Just as Tatiana had feared, Fredy's trip to Cuba was turning out to be yet another failure. For the purposes of his research and his book, at least. Aylín was much more focused on finalizing all the marriage paperwork that would, after they had fulfilled the last few requirements, allow her to legally flee her country. Fredy felt as if he were going around in circles, without achieving anything concrete. The supposed contact, somebody close to the medical team that was looking after Chávez, turned out to be a hesitant paramedic, who promised every day to have something by tomorrow and who, each morning, would offer a new promise, a new "by tomorrow." He said he was being watched, that he couldn't speak freely.

He asked for time and patience. Fredy, meanwhile, was rapidly losing both.

Day-to-day life with Aylín wasn't easy. She shared an apartment with her mother, her two children, her brother Omar, her brother Omar's wife, and a cousin called Mirtha—the journalist still hadn't figured out where she came from, nor why she lived with them. There were only three rooms. He never found out exactly where Mirtha slept. She got back late and left early. One time he got up in the middle of the night to get some water and he saw her sitting on an old wire chair. She was smoking a cigarette and she was naked. She seemed to be enthralled by the shadows. She didn't even notice him. Fredy guessed that maybe she was on drugs. He kept on walking, got himself a glass of water and went back to the room. Aylín was snoring.

But worst of all was having to fake the life of newly-weds, full of happy affection, in front of her family, the next-door neighbors, the block, the entire neighborhood, the revolution. Sometimes, when they were walking down the street, Aylín would hold his hand and rest her head on his shoulder. Fredy felt ridiculous. He thought Aylín was exaggerating. She was permanently on the lookout for spies and informers. She always thought that there might be a pair of staring eyes watching them, no matter where they were.

"Didn't you ever get married, kiddo? Haven't you ever been in love?" she asked him.

One night, shut up in the little room they were sharing, him trying to write and her shaving her legs, Aylín began to moan and say things as if they were making love, practically mimicking a low-budget tropical porno.

"Yes, Fredy, yes, just like that! Yes, yes, baby, give it to me hard!"

The journalist immediately turned to look at her, astonished. She smiled and gestured for him to calm down, to carry on writing. She wasn't actually shouting, but her voice drifted throughout the apartment; it was a subtle yet necessary performance. This, at least, was what she told him later that same night, when the others were all asleep and they could argue in hushed voices.

"It's your family! Why don't you trust them?" whispered Fredy, annoyed.

"Here, you never know."

"I can't believe this. It's incredible."

"Don't be like that. In any case, it's good to get them talking. You know, my sister-in-law will go and tell the neighbor, and then she'll tell someone else, and then that someone else will tell their husband, and on it goes. . . . Eventually everyone will know that you and I are fucking like bunnies, so nobody will suspect a thing."

Fredy continued to be amazed by all the different ways of living with fear that Aylín practiced daily. To be a citizen was, in one way or another, to be a suspect. Without alarms, theatricals, or much conflict. Distrust had become a version of sincerity. Anyone could inform on anyone else. Everyone was pre-guilty, a potential traitor. As the days went on, Fredy Lecuna started to feel more and more corralled and impotent. There was no way of getting close to the CIMEQ. He had no chance of verifying anything, of investigating, of getting hold of any information at all.

"Relax. Just calm down," Aylín would say, day after day. "The guy will talk."

But by now Fredy Lecuna had used up all his reserves of patience. A constant internal agitation meant he couldn't write. He watched as the hours withered away along with his fingers and he couldn't do a thing about it; he still hadn't come up with the first sentence of the book. He had typed up all his interviews. However little or much original work he could offer was already there, organized, ready to go. The information, the statements, the stories . . . The material was incomplete, it certainly wasn't groundbreaking, but he had run out of time. He couldn't keep waiting for the shimmering promise of the contact, who did nothing but stall and would probably never deliver. The only option he had left was to start writing. The next step was just language. After all, what was a book if not language? Words arranged one after the other, in different ways, with distinct musicality but nothing else, that was all there was to it.

He couldn't do it. It just wasn't there. He was becoming more and more irritated. He wanted to punch someone. Or maybe he just wanted to punch the words. Grab language by the throat and squeeze and shake it until it choked.

It was in the early hours of February 18, 2013, that the catastrophe occurred. Hugo Chávez returned to Caracas and Fredy Lecuna was still in Havana. He heard the news as soon as he woke up. It was the hot gossip of the day. That was when Omar came out with the saying that, on an island, the only really important news is who's just arrived and who's leaving.

"You can't leave yet, *papi*. I've still got one document to sort out and you have to sign it."

The journalist began to feel that his life was a nightmare that was chasing its own tail. Aylín promised him everything would be sorted out soon and that the supposed paramedic from the CIMEQ would finally talk to him. Ten days went by and nothing changed.

"The clocks are slower in Cuba," said Omar.

By the time March came around, Fredy was feeling desperate and escaped for an entire afternoon to the house of Jean Louis Bertrand, a correspondent for Radio France whom he had met in Old Havana and with whom he had already shared several bottles of rum and more than one tale of woe. As soon as it got dark, he used the Frenchman's telephone to call Caracas. He needed to speak to Tatiana. He hadn't heard from her, he hadn't been able to get in touch. He was worried something might have happened. He tried her mobile and couldn't get through. Then he dialed their landline. The telephone rang a few times until a woman's voice said hello.

Fredy was silent for a moment. He wasn't sure it was Tatiana's voice. He also heard, or thought he heard, other voices. And in the background music that sounded like cumbia.

"Is Tatiana there?" he asked, doubtfully, almost certain the call had been diverted to a different number.

The voice said no, that she wasn't there. And then yes, that she was there. And then it explained that she was there but not there. And then there was a muffled laugh. The woman he was speaking to was not sober, Fredy thought.

"Who's calling?"

"It's her husband," said Fredy. Gruff, serious, strained.

"It's the husband!"

And then he heard a chorus of raucous laughter. And afterward: more laughing, women's voices, loud music, and clinking ice cubes.

Andreína Mijares knew about the journalist's trip from the very start. She had managed to turn the concierge into an ally and, as soon as the concierge found out, she rang Andreína to tell her. Andreína thanked her and immediately got in touch with Virginia and delivered the news. They met up that same afternoon in a café in La California Norte. Virginia arrived with Dusty. They both agreed: it was the perfect moment to act. They had already agreed on the money. Andreína handed them the first payment that afternoon. In cash and inside a duffle bag. Just as they had requested.

"When are you going to go to the apartment?" she asked, nervously.

The two women glanced at each other.

"In a few days," said Virginia.

"But we're not going alone," Dusty pointed out, as always with a trace of sarcasm on her lips. "You're coming with us."

"Me?"

"Of course. We're just your backup team. But you're the one doing all this. You're going to break in, I mean. Or more like you're going to break into your own place, you understand?"

The following Thursday Andreína was outside the main door, waiting for them. The three women showed up late. For Andreína the wait had felt eternal, as is usually the case in life and in books. Andreína had been wringing out every minute, full of uncertainty, asking herself if the attack she was about to carry out was unjustifiable madness or simply the only sensible option left. At times, it seemed ludicrous and outrageous that, in order to defend her rights, she had to commit a crime. A crime against herself, as well as against her own property. She felt cornered by an absurd play on words. It made no sense that the only way to obey the law was by breaking the law. Uncertainty is a form of violence, too. She was on the brink of having a breakdown when Virginia, Mildred, and Dusty appeared in front of her. One was carrying a large bag; another, several smaller bags; and the third had a rucksack on her back. The three of them were smiling, and, in stark contrast to the mood of the woman who had hired them, seemed quite calm and relaxed. They had told Andreína that it would be best to act during the day, at a time when no one was inside the property. They asked her to find out the ideal time to carry out "the entrance." Andreína fulfilled her task and at ten o'clock in the morning on March 1, the four women entered apartment 34. Tatiana was at work, Fredy was away, and the little boy had gone to school. Andreína felt a peculiar emotion as she walked freely around the apartment's various spaces. Her eyes, rather than looking, seemed to be recovering each and every detail: the master bedroom window with its view of the canopy of the old mango tree that grew at the building's southern corner; the little bathroom's granite floor; the green tiles she hated so much and had envisaged changing so often; the well-worn wood of the closet in the hallway. It all came rushing back to her normal field of vision, to what ought to be a familiar, everyday view of her life. The other women did a less sentimental and more efficient circuit. They positioned themselves in each room, exchanging comments that were incomprehensible to Andreína. Dusty only paused when she got to the wardrobe in the master bedroom. She fingered the fabric of some of the dresses. Pulled open a few drawers. Took out a couple of G-strings in gaudy colors and showed them to the others. They laughed. In the bathrooms, they turned on the taps and let the water run. They found the fuse box in the kitchen and figured out which switch controlled which light in each area of the apartment. Eventually, they sat down in the dining room and fell silent. Andreína went over to them, her timid curiosity gathering strength.

"What now?"

"Now we wait," said Virginia.

Dusty brought a bottle of vodka over from the minibar.

"We're going to wait for your tenant to get back," said Mildred.

Andreína sat down next to her.

"And then?"

Virginia picked up a large picture frame in which a photograph of Fredy Lecuna was trapped beneath the glass. He was younger, with a mustache and unruly hair, smiling on a beach.

"Is this the charmer who's away on a trip?" she asked.

Andreína said that it was, and picked up the photograph, putting it back in its place. She was nervous.

"What's the plan?" she insisted.

"We're going to make her life impossible. Until she can't take it anymore. Until she leaves. That is the only plan."

The only thing she found odd at first was the smell of fried pork. She noticed it just after putting her key in the lock. It was a smell that seemed to be floating all around them. Can you smell pork? she asked Rodrigo. Or perhaps that wasn't exactly what she said. Perhaps, rather than asking, she simply commented: It smells of fried pork. How strange. And she probably also peered down the hallway toward the next-door apartment and thought that maybe they were cooking some kind of special dinner. As she turned the key in the lock, she got as far as asking herself why the smell was so strong and seemed to be coming from inside her own apartment. She opened the door and saw a dark-skinned woman, wearing cropped trousers and a red top with the outline of Chávez's profile stretched across her breasts. She was also wearing plastic flip-flops of an indeterminate color, not quite brown but not yellow either, it didn't fit into the category of sand and neither did it manage to be pale gold with any degree of conviction. She was sitting at the table, her legs wide apart. As soon as she noticed Tatiana and Rodrigo had arrived, a broad smile spread across her face and she shouted out: "They're here!" Tatiana didn't move an inch, she did not go into the apartment. She managed only to close the door. It was an instant reaction. Sudden. She and Rodrigo looked at one another in astonishment. For a second, they had a fleeting fantasy that, because of some narrative error, they had stepped into another story, somebody else's story. They stared hard at the metal number nailed to the door. There was no doubt about it. It was 34. Tatiana looked carefully at her key: more definitive proof.

"Who's that woman?" Rodrigo asked.

"I have no idea," Tatiana said.

By now it was clear that the tantalizing smell of sizzling pork shank was coming from within their own apartment. It took Tatiana only a few seconds to guess that Andreína Mijares had something to do with what was happening. When she opened the door again, this time with more caution and suspicion, there was no longer one woman there but three. Virginia hadn't moved, her outfit and position were unchanged. To one side of her was Mildred, a bandana wrapped around her head and a knife pointing straight up in her left hand. On the other side of Virginia, in a simple light-blue cotton dress through which the outline of her underwear was just visible, was Dusty. She looked as if she had just stepped out of the shower, as if she'd been interrupted halfway through the task of drying and combing her hair. Dangling listlessly from her fingers was the air rifle, and she was looking toward the doorway with irritation, as if she was wondering what these strangers were waiting for, why they wouldn't just come in. Tatiana and Rodrigo remained standing in the doorway, completely paralyzed by surprise. The smell of pork dominated the living room.

"Hi!" exclaimed Virginia with a smile. "We've been waiting for you!"

Tatiana took a few seconds to realize what was going on, to fully understand it. The three women invited her in and said hello to the boy, with insulting ease. But when she saw Andreína Mijares walk in from the back of the apartment, also fresh from a shower, she no longer required any kind of epiphany. She understood immediately that the owner had chosen to occupy the property. She was faced not with a declaration of war but with war itself. Tatiana didn't even greet her. With a snort, she took Rodrigo by the hand and headed down the hall to where the bedrooms were. Rodrigo's room was intact. Tatiana sat him down on the bed and said with absolute gravity:

"When I leave the room," she said, "you're to close the door and lock it. And you're not to open it to anyone, unless it's me, and you hear my voice loud and clear."

The boy nodded a few times, his eyes very wide. Then he asked if he could go to the toilet. His mother thought about this for a few seconds and then said he'd better not. Not yet. And she left. They had gone into her room. It was obvious. There were even a couple of items of clothing strewn across the bed, two of the dresser drawers had been pulled out, and three different jars of cream had been opened and left carelessly by the washbasin. She looked at herself in the mirror, started counting, but couldn't get further than seven. She tried to think quickly but couldn't do that either. She couldn't do anything other than shout and argue. She felt seized, or in fact possessed, by an acrid green rage at this situation that she considered as preposterous as it was unacceptable. When she went and stood in the living room, the women were eating fried pork.

"What is the meaning of all this?" she asked, looking straight at Andreína.

The other three women carried on completely unperturbed. They were chewing noisily, as if they were being paid a bonus for each extra crunch, for each letter of the alphabet they crushed along with the food between their teeth. Andreína explained that Tatiana had left her with no choice, that she didn't have anywhere else to live either and had decided to return home. She also introduced Tatiana to her three new friends, whom she had courteously invited to spend a few days with her, sharing her apartment. Virginia said pleased to meet you. Mildred made some comment about the kitchen. Dusty belched, discreetly but with a smile, a clearly calculated attempt to provoke her.

"I can't believe you're really doing this, Andreína. And with these people."

The three women glanced at each other and carried on eating. Her adversary's maddening gaze began to make Andreína feel uncomfortable.

"There's a minor living here, you know that."

Andreína looked down at her plate.

"Could we talk alone for a moment, Andreína?"

She looked up slightly and saw Virginia shaking her head from side to side in response, as if slowly stretching out the dough of an enormous, sticky "no." Tatiana snorted like a horse in the middle of winter. But winter was about as remote as a sense of calm.

"I could call the police."

"You don't say!" The three words burst right out of Dusty along with a harsh laugh. The other two only smirked. Dusty looked at her in defiance. "Have you got the number? I'll give it to you if you want."

Andreína stayed quiet, avoiding Tatiana's eyes. But even though she couldn't see her, she could still feel the other woman's gaze upon her head. Her eyes were hot. They felt as heavy as stones.

Tatiana decided that she just had to get through the first night, and that the following day she could resolve the situation by going to one of the municipality's magistrate courts or by reporting it directly to the relevant authorities. She went into the kitchen to find a disgusting mess. There was pork fat everywhere, even smeared on the refrigerator door handle. There were dirty plates on every surface. They had thrown napkins and empty cans of beer all over the floor. She took whatever she could from the fridge and emerged with a bottle of water, a piece of bread, and some leftover ham and cheese she had found.

"Hey!" Virginia said loudly and raised her hand up in the air.

Tatiana froze but didn't turn around to look at her. She gripped the food she was carrying even harder. Virginia looked at her for a few seconds, as if she were evaluating every tiny reaction.

"Us two," Virginia said, pointing at Mildred and then at herself, "are going to sleep in the master bedroom. She—" her finger drew an invisible line toward Andreína—"and Dusty—" pointing at the other woman—"will sleep here in the living room. You'll have to sleep with your son."

Tatiana felt a heavy slick of saliva slip down her throat. She just about managed to turn and look at Andreína over her shoulder.

"You're crazy," she muttered.

And she carried on walking down the hall toward the bedrooms. As soon as she had walked off, the other three women gave each other high fives, slapping their hands together in celebration.

"Turn the music up!"

Ten years old and a mirror. María was wearing a pair of blue shorts and an orange cotton T-shirt. She was standing in front of the mirror behind her mother's bedroom door. Suddenly, she felt she was taller. She looked at her unruly strands of hair, sticking out untidily in all directions. She ran her hand through it, her splayed fingers separating her hair into sections. Then she noticed her face. She moved a bit closer. She looked carefully at her features, reflected in the glass. Her eyes were black, restless. Her lips were small, her nose round, buttonlike. Her ears—were they very big? She put her hands over them. She moved a little closer. Until she could feel the mirror's cold breath on her skin. Were they very big? She took her hands away. She looked at them again.

Your hair is a mess, María. She heard her mother's voice without hearing it.

How could she go and meet her boyfriend looking like this? She allowed her eyes to run slowly down her body. Her T-shirt was old. Her shorts were a little too small, a bit tight. Her bare feet looked as if they were nailed to the floor. Her eyes once again. She took a step back, looking at herself. She raised her arms and, in one quick movement, took off her T-shirt. She let it fall to one side, without taking her eyes off her eyes in the mirror. For a moment she was scared, she didn't dare look at herself. Then she slowly extended her gaze, stretching it out, timidly, fearfully, trying to get her whole body to fit within her gaze.

Her breasts. Small and flat. A child's breasts. She looked at her belly button, too. Just before her fingers undid the button on her shorts and pushed them downward, straining a little. The fabric fell to her ankles. Her eyes again. Meanwhile, she kicked the shorts away. Her eyes traveled across her slender figure again. Her white underwear. Not one ring in her ears. Were they really big, her ears? Ten years old and a mirror. A naked little girl. More alone than ever.

María started trying on her mother's clothes. At first she did so sheepishly, almost as if she were playing a game, a trivial act, a spontaneous event. The wardrobe door was ajar and she suddenly glimpsed, through the crack, the lilac blouse with the little wooden buttons. Her mother loved that shirt. She never said so but it was obvious given how often she used to wear it. It was the one she almost always put on whenever they went out. On the street, anyone who had seen her more than once might have thought it was the only blouse she owned. It was a strong lilac, it had character. It was a single piece of fabric; the buttons were just for decoration. María climbed up onto a chair to reach the hanger. She could have just pulled the blouse down but instead she chose to take it over to the mirror on its hanger and hold it up against her shoulders. She looked at herself. Then she hung it from the door handle and undressed quickly, with a childlike emotion she hadn't felt for a long time. As if she were about to receive a gift. The fabric slid over her skin until it reached her knees. María adjusted the neck first, trying to hold a posture that would leave her collarbones visible, and then she tried to tie the material in a knot so it came in around her waist. She tried to transform the blouse into a dress. She tried to make it give her body more shape. She leaned over to the left, practically hanging in midair, bending her hips a little and gazed at her reflection for a moment, frozen in the mirror.

A second or two later she collapsed, she couldn't help laughing, a tiny yet manic laugh that seemed to have been trapped somewhere inside her body for a very long time: a laugh that gradually fell out of her, that didn't want to stop, that turned all at once into a twirl, a dance in front of the mirror, a grin, the wild repetition of a ten-year-old's silliness within the glass. She ended up sitting on the floor, leaning back against her mother's bed, looking at her reflection, that piece of lilac cloth like a flag wrapped around her body: her dirty knees peeping out from between the folds of the garment, and higher up and further back, her face, her eyes wet and shining, her smile. She could hear the television in the background. But she wasn't listening to it. It was like a washing machine that was always running. She got up, opened her mother's wardrobe, ran her eyes over its contents, and started to pull out the clothes. All of them.

Ten years: María, naked, wobbling in a pair of high heels. Trying to balance, her hands outstretched. In fits of laughter.

That night, Rodrigo was finally able to get back online. Dr. Sanabria gave him his Wi-Fi password and the boy thanked him. I'm not hungry, he added. And then he blurted out a "goodnight" and he almost definitely said "thank you" again, before rushing into the bedroom that Sanabria had tidied up for him and closing the door. He felt anxious, uneasy. The situation in his house was troubling and incomprehensible to him. He didn't really understand what was going on and found it even harder to tell what was going to happen next. But it seemed all wrong. Maybe this was also why, when he thought about his date, the whole process leading up to it seemed ridiculous and childish. Having no name is not good, he thought. Being called Vampire seemed silly. And the name Butterfly annoyed him too. At that moment, he thought butterflies were pathetic.

He sat down in front of his laptop and started looking for his girlfriend in all the chat room's dark corners. María had been waiting for him for more than half an hour. She had gone from feeling nervous to distressed. All the excitement that had been gradually building as she had gotten dressed and prepared the room had turned into a mild sense of frustration. She felt ridiculous, sitting in the darkness wearing one of her mother's blouses, clipped at the back with a clothes peg. She'd also put on the blue earrings, and dangling from her left wrist was the bracelet that completed the outfit. In front of the mirror in her mother's room she had spent a long time trying to put her hair up in a bun, a new hairstyle, one that would make her look different. She had put lipstick on. And makeup. She had even sprayed a little perfume on her neck. It was her first date, the first date she had ever been on.

When she heard the ringing sound and saw that Vampire was calling her, she hesitated. For a second, the idea—or the urge—to run from the room flushed through her. She looked down at her feet: she had put on her mother's high heels, too.

"Hi! Are you there?" Vampire whispered. It was obvious that María's dark bedroom meant he couldn't see a thing.

"I'm here," she said, huddled in the chair, staring at the image of Rodrigo on her computer screen.

She liked him. She watched him lean forward toward her, toward his own screen, squinting, trying to find her. She liked his face, his small eyes, the spiky hair just above his forehead. She thought he looked really nice. And she was pleased she liked the look of him, her boyfriend.

"But I can't see you!" Rodrigo cried.

"And I can't hear you!" she lied, smiling now.

"You can't hear me? Really?"

"Now I can."

"I didn't realize how late it was," he said, sadly. "There's a problem at home. It's a bit complicated, I'll tell you about it later."

They were both quiet for a moment. Rodrigo moved his screen, checked the connection of one of the cables, stared hard into the depths of the screen. All he could see was a dark shape that sometimes also looked like a silhouette. The glittering bracelet briefly lit up the right-hand corner of the computer.

"You don't want me to see you? Is that it?"

María chewed her lip.

"Because you can see me, can't you?"

Another pause. Taut.

"Are you looking at me right now?"

María held her breath. She felt as if everything was on the verge of plunging into a precipice and disappearing. In an impulsive movement, a little abrupt, she pressed the switch on the old standard floor lamp next to the computer. The clinical white of the incandescent bulb flooded her room. Little by little, the shape and the colors of her body grew clearer on Rodrigo's computer screen.

"Here I am," she mumbled, trying to keep a lid on her fear. "Can you see me now?"

Rodrigo nodded slowly, as he stared at the image of Butterfly. He looked impressed.

"Is that you?" he asked.

She confirmed that it was, nodding her head and feeling, at the same time, as if a hedgehog were burying itself in her throat.

"Are you wearing a costume?" Rodrigo said next, no longer hiding his surprise.

María prickled with shame. She reached out and switched off the lamp with a smack, and jumped up in an attempt to stand, but her mother's shoes got the better of her. She wobbled for a couple of seconds, her outline shaking on the screen, then she came crashing down, noisily. As she dragged herself along, pushing herself forward with her elbows and walking on her knees, she heard Rodrigo's voice calling her.

"Woah! Hey! What happened?"

In the bathroom, as hastily and clumsily as before, María tried to pull off all her mother's clothes, mess up her hair so it looked as natural as possible, take off her lipstick and wipe away all the makeup. When she returned, almost panting, she looked radically different. Vampire was still looking around, peering into the darkness, trying to find her.

"There," said María. "I'm back."

She sat and waited, sensing Rodrigo trying to scrutinize her again.

"You have to turn the light on," he said.

She realized she was still sitting in the dark. She took a deep breath and switched the lamp on again. At last they were looking at one another. Rodrigo found María's messy hair amusing. He also liked the whitish-blue mark visible on her left cheek. And the fact that she had one lip redder than the other. He loved that. She watched him looking at her and knew that he liked what he saw. They spent a few moments in silence, examining one another. Then they looked into each other's eyes. Shyly, uneasily, but happily.

"I don't want to call you Butterfly anymore. I don't like it."

"And I don't want to call you Vampire. It's silly."

"My name's Rodrigo."

"Mine's María."

"The problem isn't your neighbors. The problem is you."
This was his brother's response to his various sorrows.

Miguel had gone to visit him and told him about everything that was going on in his building. From Antonio's point of view, letting the boy into his house had been his first mistake.

"What was I supposed to do? The husband's away, their family lives in Maturín, and she was standing there, crying, totally overwhelmed."

"The point is, you've now brought that war into your own house. You've made it worse."

"The boy's no trouble. He's quiet."

Antonio simply made a face and poured out coffee into one cup and tea into another. Miguel had an ulterior motive for visiting. He needed to find Vladimir. Even though he knew the relationship between father and son wasn't exactly perfect, he hoped that Antonio would know something, be able to offer some clue. His nephew had vanished, disappeared off the face of the earth, and the American journalist had already called him a couple of times. He had not answered. Nor had he returned the call. But he remembered his promise to Vladimir. She was the one to whom he was supposed to hand over the mobile, with the videos on it, should the situation arise. Sanabria just wanted to confirm that this instruction still held. Did he really want this gringa to see those images? Was it really necessary?

Less than half an hour had gone by when the two

brothers started talking about Chávez. Talking about anything else felt forced.

"There's a whole campaign financed by the gringos," Antonio said. "They're manipulating everything to do with his illness to make people anxious. It's psychological warfare, pure and simple."

Miguel didn't know how to respond to such suggestions. He felt like they relied on two different versions of logic, foreign to one another.

"This is a global conflict, Miguel. And we're in the middle of it. The future of humanity's being decided here. The two economic models are up against each other here. We are now the number one enemy of international capitalism."

"Who is 'we'?"

"Us, damn it, Venezuelans!" replied Antonio. And then he seemed to feel obliged to clarify: "The revolutionary Venezuelans! The majority!" he concluded, exasperated.

"We're all going mad here, Antonio."

Miguel was irritated and depressed by the growing religiousness that had been creeping over the government during the first few months of 2013. He found the idolization of the president harder and harder to bear. People spoke about Chávez as if he were the reincarnation of Simón Bolívar.

"You've been very irritable for a while now, Miguel. You're turning into a radical."

"I'm just defending myself from you lot. I can't stand what you're doing. You're already saying that Chávez gave his life for us."

"And how is that not the case?"

"Oh, come on!"

Some actually believed that Chávez's illness was punishment for having dared to provoke death. Some believed that all of this was to do with the curse that had been unleashed a few years earlier, between July 15 and 16, 2010. At first, only the insomniacs found out. That morning, the president posted a message on his social media account, announcing that Simón Bolívar's body was being exhumed. A few hours later, in a transmission across the country's media outlets, Chávez himself confirmed the news and presented a video, describing the experience as he went. Experts and officials wearing special, completely airtight suits, surrounded the leader in a session that people said had gone on for nineteen hours. They were all standing next to the Liberator's open coffin, hovering around the remains of the country's founding father. Shadows among shadows. "Last night," Chávez said, "looking at him, I asked him silently, in prayer: 'Father, is that you?' And he replied like Pablo Neruda himself, straight from the heart: 'Yes, it's me, but I wake up once every hundred years.'" And so, the legend was born. No one touches Bolívar's bones and remains intact. Anyone who disturbs the remains of a body shall be eternally punished.

Death is contagious, too.

Popular tradition holds that it is not healthy to sniff around the deceased. That includes language, too. Death is a tedious word. It sticks to your fingers, gets tangled up, irritates. Once you have touched it, it is very hard to get rid of it. It is always wise to keep your distance. But official rhetoric, for too many years, did the opposite. It flirted with the word. It used it and recycled it ad nauseum. It was present in speeches and slogans with dogged consistency. "Homeland or death!" El

Comandante would shout. "We shall overcome!" the inflamed multitude would howl in response. It was part of the continental left's heritage. And the government had squeezed every last drop from it, with pride and pleasure. It had even gone so far as to institutionalize it: in 2007, Chávez signed an official memo declaring the slogan "Homeland, socialism or death!" a form of greeting among members of the military as they went about their official duties. It was about symbolically giving form to an epic, the epic that was so painfully absent from the self-proclaimed Bolivarian revolution. Chávez had not overthrown a dictator. He had not fought an invasion. But he spoke as if he were Che Guevara, as if he belonged to the league of the great Latin American freedom fighters. The temperature of his rhetoric was above and beyond his reality: all he had done was win an election in an oil-rich country. He had never faced imminent danger during military action. He was a public official, not a warrior.

His combative discourse, hell-bent on defying death, began to peel away when the illness suddenly appeared. The slogans changed, the word "death" began to be avoided, an attempt was made to twist the symbols: overcome and live, live forever, a free homeland, and never die.

In the beginning was the word, and then the word founded a church.

This is how it happened. Throughout 2012, Chávez gradually built himself up as a religious figure. At the end of the year, in a message read out to the army, he wrote: "The people of Simón Bolívar are the light of the world." His church started to professionalize in 2013. Very soon, people began talking about Chávez as the redeemer of the poor, martyr of the oppressed. Ceremonial rhetoric announcing the definitive creation of a new congregation began to seep into political discourse. "In his name, through him and in him," the vice president once said, alluding of course to El Comandante. The new slogans were already pointing toward the heavens: "Let us be like Bolívar! Let us be like Chávez!" The mute president, his voice silenced, began to be replaced by myth. In this land of symbols, the real Chávez was dying. The sick man was becoming less and less sick, and increasingly an image without a body: a sacred image. The crude, irascible, authoritarian, and whimsical Chávez was fading away, giving way to a new fictional character, a fetish. The cancer could only be cured with a sacrament. Mystic marketing launched its latest religious product: here is the Christ of the poor.

And, then, the miracle of the multiplication of the adjectives occurred:

Colossal

Gigantic

Bright

Supreme

Guiding

Unique

Immense

Holy

Undefeated

Superior

Eternal

Immortal

Celestial

Universal

Galactic

Alone or in combination, multi-use, detachable, placed next to any noun, cultivated and reproduced with multiple variables, large-scale distribution, high-frequency, repeated to the infinite great beyond, which was also the immaculate space where, from that moment onward and forever more, El Comandante would live and breathe.

"You still don't get it, Miguel. I'm being serious. We're talking about an extraordinary man, a guy on the same level as Bolívar."

"Oh, for fuck's sake. Chávez is such an egomaniac that he couldn't bear to be alone in his sickness: he had to go and infect the rest of the country," snarled Sanabria.

"Say what you like. Many of you wish he would just die, but, when he does, you're going to miss him. Remember that."

"We're not going to miss anything. The military will still be in charge. You know it's true. This is just a return to what this country's always been: an army barracks."

Antonio belonged to the old guard of the left, which, within government circles, stood in opposition to the military men, many of whom had trained alongside the president. Whenever his brother mentioned the army, Antonio would immediately try to change the subject, attempting to dodge the issue, suddenly recalling one of his personal woes and trying to shift the conversation elsewhere. Their conversation would go something like this: Did you hear about the national treasurer? Miguel would ask. He's ex-military, Miguel would say, answering his own question. They say he's got more than four billion dollars now. A personal friend of Chávez, by the way, he would add. Apparently, he's the one who handles his private accounts. And Antonio would retort: Two days ago, I woke up smelling of fish, isn't that strange? Miguel would carry on: And you can't pretend you don't know what's happening, with all the reports that have been filed against the military mafia. That's who's controlling the foreign exchange. The government itself admits that more than twenty billion dollars have disappeared. What do you make of that? Antonio would then reply: I woke up and it seemed as though the pillow were covered in fish, as if it were a net, and inside there were feathers and sardines, feathers and horse mackerel, salmon and feathers. And Miguel: Do you know how many military men are ministers or governors or hold key public posts? Do you remember last year when Chávez said that this was "a military revolution"? Do you think that's a good thing? And Antonio: I took all the tests, it's not like I'm a compulsive hypochondriac or anything. I know, I know. There's nothing wrong with me, I'm old, but even so, I swear that I woke up smelling like that, what do you make of it? And Miguel: Damn it, are you listening to me? And Antonio: Damn it, are you listening to me?

Then they sat in silence for a while. As if letting their moods recover the capacity for fondness they had for one another. Antonio asked after Beatriz and the new grandchild. Miguel told him that all was well, that the child would be born in March. And he seized his chance, now that they had moved on to a new topic, the sphere of family inquiries, to ask about Vladimir.

"I'm worried," said Antonio. "Has he not been in touch with you?"

"No. I've not heard from him in a long time."

"He was here in December," said Antonio. "Then in January he went back to Cuba. And I haven't heard a thing since then."

"But you know he's in the country, at least?" asked Miguel, trying to conceal his anxiety.

"I suppose so, but I can't be sure. Chávez came back. What reason would Vladimir have to stay in Cuba?"

Miguel nodded and sipped at the last of his tea. Antonio scratched his head. He didn't seem overly worried.

"Are you," he said, looking at his brother curiously, "looking for him for any particular reason?"

"No, no," lied Miguel.

He remembered the words and images of Chávez in the video. And his tea suddenly tasted like aluminium.

"There's a Cuban at the door!" whispered the concierge.

But it was a whisper that contained a shout, an urgency that was also visible in her expression. She had decided not to inform him via the intercom or the telephone. Instead, she had come up, knocked on the door, and quickly delivered this strained whisper.

Dr. Sanabria felt an icy spark, a drop of freezing water rapidly snaking its way from the depths of his gut to halfway up his throat.

A Cuban at the door.

The concierge's sentence floated in the air. Sanabria saw it, felt it quiver, like an insect in the air. The concierge quickly told him everything.

"The man was pressing some of the buttons on the intercom as I was just arriving. He said that he'd been told that there was an apartment to rent in the building. Asked me if it was true. If I knew which one it was. I recognized his accent as soon as I heard him speak. And I said to myself: He's trying to play dumb, but this son of a bitch is Cuban. And I said: No one's renting anything out here. And I said it just like that, sternly. So he'd understand that we were all opposition here."

The woman paused for a moment, as if waiting for an ideological affirmation, some sign of approval.

Sanabria felt obliged to give her a conspiratorial wink. She went on:

"I got a bad feeling about the guy. He looked like a cop. Then he started telling me a weird story. He said he'd gotten the wrong building, that it must be a different one, that this one here was actually where a friend of his was living, that was it. And he tried to joke around, you know, Cuban-style, trying to be charming, but I didn't laugh at all and he started asking me all these odd questions, I felt like he was trying to find out stuff about the people who live in the building. And then I squared up to him, all serious, and I said: I'm not authorized to provide that information, sir. Just like that. With this same look on my face."

Sanabria immediately thought of his nephew. A nervous Vladimir, warning him. Be careful.

The concierge, meanwhile, had already moved on to another topic, what was happening in apartment 34. All the neighbors were complaining about the noise. It was unprecedented. She wanted to know if Sanabria was aware, and he gave her no details, only said that yes, he was aware. The woman had no option but to return to the topic of the Cuban:

"We've got to be careful," she pointed out. "I heard about this on the radio. They say that the whole thing about Chávez being ill is a lie. That in Cuba they brainwashed him and now they've kidnapped him. That these people are determined to invade this country."

Once he was alone again, Sanabria sat down in front of his bookshelves and tried to calm his nerves. He supposed that the man who had been prowling around the building could easily be a Cuban security official. He was certain that his presence was related to Vladimir's absence. His nephew still had not shown up. It was feasible, therefore, that something had happened.

Difficulties of language: too many things could fit inside the word "something."

It was feasible, therefore, to imagine that the intelligence agencies of both governments had discovered what his nephew was hiding and so were following the trail of the mobile phone and the videos. His adrenaline levels shot up. He recalled what Vladimir had asked him to do. He remembered his orders: if a Cuban shows up, he should throw the box away, get rid of everything. He looked at his bookshelves. The box of cigars was sitting slightly askew on top of some books. He thought of the American journalist, too. His nephew had assured him that she could be trusted. What should he do? What should he do with the last words of El Comandante?

The art of disappearance is cruel and paradoxical. Disappearing someone else is easier than disappearing oneself. No one ever manages to vanish completely. Sooner rather than later the police pieced the clues together and contacted María's family in San Cristóbal. March was just beginning. Cecilia, her godmother, was the angriest of all. She felt personally betrayed. What's more, she couldn't understand how the girl had been able to establish and sustain the lie for such a long time. Her punishment would be severe.

María sat down on the sofa in the living room, practically underneath the blaring television set. She thought she was going to cry but she didn't; she was actually more angry than she was upset. Then she went to her room, to the computer, to that little square of light where she could look urgently for her boyfriend.

As for Rodrigo, there was no way he was ever going to feel relaxed in Miguel Sanabria's house. No matter how friendly and fun the doctor tried to seem, however young and adaptable, he was still an old man. His age defined him. Time makes no exceptions.

Rodrigo couldn't help feeling that he was in someone else's house, so very different, filled with different objects, and that the old man had nothing to say to him. He felt nothing more than respect for him. He knew that in this apartment he had to speak in a low voice, take excessive care, move slowly, softly, always afraid he might break something, like the air, for instance. The air's traditions. Its currents, its routines.

Beyond that, he also felt uncomfortable being held captive in the Sanabria household knowing what his mother was going through one floor below: knowing that she might be yelling, fighting, face-to-face with those other women, and at a clear disadvantage. At night, he couldn't get to sleep. He woke up constantly. He thought about his father, too. It alarmed him that they had no idea what was going on with him, and, in turn, that his father had no idea what was going on with them. All the fighting aside, Fredy was his father. Rodrigo wished he were there right then. Even with his bad moods and his stress, Rodrigo preferred him to Dr. Sanabria and his well-meaning friendship. Rodrigo was also increasingly desperate to chat with his girlfriend all the time.

That night they spoke on Skype, but only on María's condition that they not use the camera. She didn't want them to see each other. Rodrigo started to protest but quickly gave in. María was the most serious she had ever been. Her voice had an almost solemn tone. She enunciated the ends of words, using pauses that Rodrigo hadn't heard before.

"I don't want to see you," she said, "because I've got to tell you something awful."

Rodrigo feared a breakup. He didn't dare ask her what it was about. But María told him. She explained that she had lied, that she hadn't told him the truth about her mother. Her mother, obliterated on the pavement of an ordinary street. Her mother, with two bullets in her body. Her mother, clinging for all eternity to her handbag. Her mother, who heard the words "old bitch" and two shots.

Her mother, who fell to the ground without seeing María. Who let go of her hand and disappeared.

"My mother's dead," she said, her voice breaking. "She was killed. And I never told you."

Rodrigo felt as if he had a hot bubble of air stuck behind his ribs. He thought he could hear María crying. And he didn't know how to reply, what to say.

And then she carried on talking. She told him more. She told him about her solitary existence during that brief period of time. Her little lies, her big lies, her loneliness, her not-knowing-what-to-do. She told him that, at first, she didn't tell him anything, she didn't know how to, and then later she still didn't tell him anything because she didn't know how he would react. She didn't want to lose him. He was all she really had.

The corners of his eyes were stinging. As if he had vinegar on his eyelids.

They sat there in silence for a few seconds, until she admitted that she had been found out. That in the end her godmother and the rest of the family had discovered the truth. The criminal investigators eventually found the clue they needed. Cecilia had telephoned her. She was indignant, beside herself. In two days, they would come for her to take her to live with her godmother's family in San Cristóbal.

Then Rodrigo spoke. He also had a secret story to tell her. A father and a mother in the midst of a crisis. A house full of strangers. A house that was no longer his. A war they had had to flee. An apartment where he lived and did not live, where he had to walk carefully and breathe quietly so as not to break the air.

That night, Rodrigo and María decided to run away together.

Official figures continued to be scarce, erratic. On February 22, the vice president claimed to have held a five-hour meeting with Hugo Chávez. Although he had admitted that the head of state was aided by a breathing tube that meant he could not speak, he said that Chávez "communicated via various written means in order to guide us." He added that the dialogue had also been possible thanks to "various means of understanding," and that the president was still in "extraordinary spirits, he has a bright smile and lively, shining eyes." A few days later, the government insisted on denouncing a global campaign that, taking advantage of his illness, sought to destabilize the nation. On March 1, the vice president repeated the accusations and stared directly at the television camera filming him: "How far will the bourgeoisie go? Stop these attacks on El Comandante! Stop the rumors!" he shouted.

The four women were sitting watching the screen. They were eating peanuts and drinking beer.

"He can't die," Mildred murmured.

"If he does, I don't think I could take it," said Virginia.

Andreína remained stationary, inscrutable, looking at the television. The others watched her out of the corners of their eyes, waiting for some kind of reaction. It was a live transmission. The vice president continued with his rant. There is a minority that hates our country, he proclaimed. "Faced with these rumors, kneel down! Revolutionary strength! Trust! Unity!"

"You're definitely a squalid, aren't you?"

On the same day, the minister of communications denounced the existence of "a psychological operation, deployed with the purpose of generating anxiety amongst the Venezuelan people." He claimed that some people were looking to "bring about unrest" in the country using social media and phone messaging. The situation was becoming more and more disconcerting. Asking about the president's illness was no longer just sacrilege, it could now be perceived as a terrorist act. The government vilified anyone who wasn't satisfied with what they were given, with the official reports. Curiosity began to be criminalized.

The latest bulletin from the minister of communications, broadcast on national television the night of March 4 following a terse communiqué stating that the president's health was in a fragile state, delivered a lengthy political message, denouncing the "corrupt right" and declaring that the opposition would never govern the country again. And this was how the last report on the health of the patient Hugo Chávez Frías ended: "At this time, unity and discipline are the foundations for guaranteeing the country's political stability."

"You didn't answer me," said Dusty, sitting down in front of Andreína at the dining-room table.

Andreína was answering her emails. She was sitting at her laptop, a cup of coffee at her side.

"I'm not interested in politics. They irritate me."

"Did you vote for Chávez?"

"No."

"And are you happy he's sick? Do you want him to die?"

"No, of course not. I don't want anyone to die."

"But they say there are lots of people who want Chávez to die."

Andreína made a scornful face, as if condemning the people Dusty was referring to. She shifted her eyes back to the screen, in the hope that her expression would be enough to end the conversation. They were both quiet for a few minutes. But the other woman didn't move. She was still there, drinking her beer, looking at Andreína without saying a word. Andreína didn't know where to put that look, how to avoid it, how to ignore it, what to do with it. She stopped typing. She waited for a few more seconds. The silence was like a hair, thin and brittle. Finally, she accepted the challenge and turned to look at Dusty.

"So," she said all of a sudden, as if picking up the threads of a conversation they had left hanging in the air, "why do they call you that?"

"Dusty?"

Andreína nodded. She lowered her laptop screen ever so slightly.

"What's your real name?"

"Yamileth," Dusty replied. "But nobody really calls me that. Ever since I can remember, they've called me Dusty. Because we were the last ones to arrive in the neighborhood. We came from Chejendé, in Trujillo. There were no jobs there, there was nothing. And my mother had a cousin in Caracas. We got here and built ourselves a little house with planks of wood, right on top of a hill. That's where we found a spot. It was all still nothing but soil, back then. My mum's cousin's husband helped us. He found my ma a job cleaning in a school, around Mesuca.

And I stayed up there at home looking after my brothers and sisters. There were four of us. I was the eldest. I was six."

Andreína lowered her gaze. Looked at her nails. Suddenly she was embarrassed that they were so manicured, so polished.

"That's what they called all of us who lived there. We were the Dusties. Because there were no streets there, no stairs, no nothing. We were fucked. Sometimes we didn't even eat. We didn't have a fucking thing. Everything was dust. Dust and us. We were the poorest of the poor, know what I mean?"

Andreína had learned more about her country in a few days than she had in her entire life. She had spent too much time with these women. She had cooked and eaten with them. She had drunk and gotten drunk with them, too. Together, they had been cruel and aggressive toward Tatiana. Who urinated out in the corridor, in front of the door to the room where she slept? She struggled to remember. They had started with rum and ended up drinking aniseed liqueur. They listened to music. They discovered they had some favorites in common. Then Virginia had talked about her dead son, murdered. Mildred also had two siblings who had died the same way: bullets, always bullets. One in a fight at a party. The other over some trouble with drugs. Dusty changed the subject. She turned the music up and started dancing in the middle of the living room. That was the last thing she remembered. After that there were only shadows, laughter, someone knocking on the bedroom door, but there was no answer. Andreína recalled the sensation of revenge, of power. As if that moment was payback for the subjugation and humiliation she had suffered at the hands of Tatiana and her husband in the past. The way they had ignored her. How they had never replied to her messages. How they had refused to give her what was rightfully hers. Her memories were vague but gratifying, they gave her a delicious feeling of retribution. Her mind would occasionally offer up a fleeting image, shrouded in gloom. A trickle of urine streaming onto the floor. Cheers.

Did she do it? Was she really capable of doing something like that?

Destruction is also a discipline. It has an order, a plan. Sanabria had witnessed firsthand how Tatiana had lost more territory and confidence with every day that went by. Even the other residents had begun to resign themselves to the intruders' presence in apartment 34. Perhaps if this had happened at another time, thought Sanabria, everyone would have reacted differently. But any distraction seemed impossible these days. There was a strange sense of imminence in the air. A dense mood seemed to have descended over everything. It was March 5 and even the air was taut, poised to screech. The silence was a question mark.

When the high-ranking government officials appeared on television, they were all wearing the same serious expression, a collective long face, a grimace that looked almost like grief. They were gathered in the Palacio de Miraflores. The ratings were achingly inevitable: at that very moment, most Venezuelans were sitting in front of a screen, pinching the uncertainty between their fingers. Looking straight into the camera, the vice president said: "We are in no doubt whatsoever, and the moment will come when we are able to put together a scientific committee to prove this, that El Comandante was maliciously infected with this disease."

He disclosed nothing else. But his comment was an inadequate preamble. A defensive prologue. Sanabria heard the buzz of the intercom and stood up to see who it was, a little exasperated. He struggled to understand what the anxious concierge was saying to him, her voice very quiet. After a few seconds, he made out a few words from her mumbles.

"The Cuban's here again, Doctor! But now he's asking specifically for you!"

Sanabria froze. In one second, a purplish streak flashed before his eyes and flooded his vision. He guessed that his blood pressure had rocketed. He said that he would be down right away, and hung up. Then he walked quickly back to the living room and stopped in front of the bookshelves. He looked at the box.

Sanabria was not a man of action. He never had been. He picked up the box, took out the telephone and began pacing around the living room, with each step making movements he couldn't finish, indecisive, volatile. He didn't know what to do. Destroy the telephone, throw away the box? Keep it and give it to the American journalist? Finally, clumsily, bewildered, he put the wooden box back onto the uneven pile of books, on the shelf by the television.

The telephone was a dead mouse in his hand.

Sanabria spun around, his eyes darting around the room. What was stopping him from throwing the telephone down the garbage chute, or simply crushing it with his foot? Why didn't he destroy it? The questions danced anxiously around him.

The intercom buzzed again in the kitchen. It was like the buzzing of a bee.

Sanabria gave a start. Then suddenly his gaze settled on a corner of the sofa, where Rodrigo's school bag lay. In that moment, he felt it was a sign. He went over, unzipped the little boy's fabric bag, and slid the mobile inside. He thought it seemed like an innocent place. The best place to keep a secret.

Then he hurried out of the apartment.

The Cuban was a tall, well-dressed man, with good manners and a calm voice. He was only looking for information. As the concierge had refused to give him any, he had asked to speak to the representative of the residents' association. This is why he had asked for Sanabria. Sanabria was still nervous. He didn't understand what this was all about. The man explained that he had been pressing the buzzer for apartment 34 to no avail, and that he just wanted to confirm that this was citizen Fredy José Lecuna Jiménez's current residence.

The concierge, a few feet away, watched the two men. She seemed suspicious.

Sanabria said that yes, he could confirm it was, that the journalist did indeed live in that apartment. He didn't think it would be right to provide any more details, but he asked what was going on, why were they looking for Fredy Lecuna?

"It's a procedural matter. This citizen married a comrade, a volunteer worker, and we're carrying out a routine investigation."

Sanabria returned home, still disconcerted. Trying to put the following unanswered questions in order: Fredy Lecuna had gotten married? Why? Did Tatiana know? What was really going on with that family?

As soon as he went inside, he noticed its absence. Rodrigo's rucksack was no longer on the sofa. Once again, he felt an icy lightning bolt course through his body. He practically ran into the bedroom, looking for the boy. But he wasn't there either. He searched the house twice. Every corner, every nook, every cranny. Nothing. He called his mother. Rodrigo wasn't with her, either. He went back downstairs and spoke to the concierge. She didn't know anything, hadn't seen anything.

Sanabria thought that perhaps the boy had gone to a friend's house. He must have slipped out while he himself was talking to the Cuban man, but would come back soon. He decided to pour himself a whiskey and sit down in front of the television. He thought that, at that moment, the entire country was sitting in front of a television. He tried to calm himself down. All he could do was wait. His wife called from Panama.

"Is it true he's dead?" It was more of an interrogation than a question. "That's the rumor that's going around here," she added. "Everyone's saying that Chávez has bitten the dust."

Sanabria was restless, not in the mood, thinking about Rodrigo. He blurted out an answer. Said he didn't know anything. His mind was elsewhere.

"What the hell do you mean, *elsewhere*, Miguel? Turn on the television, call Vladimir, find out whatever you can. And then let me know, OK? We're all waiting for news here, you know."

A small ice cube cracked inside his glass.

Two hours later the vice president was back on national television, and he announced the death of Hugo Chávez. His voice breaking, struggling to hold back the tears, he revealed that at precisely four twenty-five that very afternoon, the body of the president had lost all signs of life.

For a few seconds, the country was silence. A tense, electric silence: a metal-filled abyss, an open vowel, a scream about to spurt blood. Until the vice president spoke again, still falteringly. He asked for respect and peace, he spoke of immortal remains, he raised his fist and shouted honor and glory, long live Hugo Chávez, may Hugo Chávez live forever.

Sanabria switched off the television. He had drunk three glasses of whiskey and felt gently tipsy. Neither happy nor sad, just fragile. Vulnerable. Beatriz rang. She told him they were all celebrating. Sanabria muttered: You know how I feel about that. She said: Don't be a killjoy, Miguel. And he replied: You shouldn't celebrate anybody's death. And she: Let's not argue again. And he: I think it's immoral, Beatriz. He's a human being. And then she started naming other deaths, people who had fallen into disgrace or ruin, fallen ill or had died, all because of the president. Do you not think that's immoral? she asked. I don't agree with any of it, he said. And she said: I can't stand you when you get like this. And he: silence. And she: more silence. Let's just speak tomorrow.

He waited for Rodrigo, he waited a long time, his feeling of dread growing with every minute that passed. He tried to distract himself and he couldn't do it. He paced around the apartment. He searched everything a thousand times. And again. And found nothing. Nothing, a thousand times. Nothing again. He sat down, stood up, started walking around again. Until night fell. Until the night grew even denser and he couldn't bear it any longer. To wait is to go mad.

"I think your son has run away."

Tatiana stared at him in astonishment. She looked lost, her eyes red, her pale face gleaming against the wide, dark shadows under her eyes. She was standing in the door to her apartment, which, strictly speaking, was no longer her apartment but rather just apartment 34: battleground.

It was ten o'clock at night. Since Chávez's death had been officially announced, the country had slipped into a disconcerting calm. Sanabria had first asked if she had heard from Rodrigo, and, faced with the boy's mother's look of surprise and shake of the head, he reluctantly explained his theory that he had run away. Together they returned to Sanabria's apartment, checked the room where the boy had been sleeping, and discovered that he had taken plenty of clothes and some of his most treasured possessions. Tatiana made several telephone calls. One after another, they added up to the same result: no one knew where her son was. Tatiana started to cry and clung to Dr. Sanabria.

"I can't take it," she murmured.

Sanabria felt her nipples press into his ribs and felt an unwanted stir, a feeling that was completely inappropriate in that moment. He was genuinely moved by the woman's sobbing, he was genuinely despairing about the disappearance of the telephone with which his nephew had entrusted him, so why did he also have to feel genuinely flustered by the physical contact, innocent and accidental? He felt ashamed. An instantaneous, almost feral shame. Tatiana, gripping him as if he were the mast of a boat, kept repeating the same words again and again.

"I can't take it."

They arranged to meet outside the metro station. They recognized each other but weren't sure how to greet one another. Rodrigo thought about giving her a kiss, a kiss on the cheek—friendly, intimate, but on the cheek. María was tempted to give him a hug. But they stood there looking at one other and simply said hello. Hello and hello: that was all. Their nerves contained, crouching down behind their words. With an unpronounceable shine in their eyes: the gleam in a gaze can never be translated into words.

"Hello," said Rodrigo.

"Hello," said María.

And all around them, the traffic continued its impassive roar. They walked to María's apartment. They climbed the stairs and stopped in front of the door. They spent the entire afternoon and part of the night in the apartment, talking. María showed him everything he needed to see. Rodrigo was fascinated by the collection of resin eyes still lying on the work surface in her mother's room. They cooked together. She made a pan of rice and they put four hot dogs in a frying pan. The television was switched off. They didn't hear about Chávez's death. They slid underneath the whole country without noticing.

Their minds were elsewhere: the following day, her godmother would arrive to pick up María and her things and take them to San Cristóbal. At ten o'clock that night they lay down on her mother's bed, side by side. Rodrigo thought the mattress was old, that it sagged far too much. María stared at the ceiling, her hands clasped over her belly button.

"Are you sure you've got everything ready?"

"Yes. I've been packing for nearly a whole week."

Rodrigo shifted a little, moved himself into a position very like the one María was in. Staring upward, his hands crossed on his stomach.

He ventured a letter. An *a* stuck to the roof of his mouth. He sounded it out for a few seconds and then immediately regretted it. It seemed he had nothing to say. It was a long "a," a seeking "a," diligently searching for the next letter to dock at.

"A . . . and, you're not sleepy?" he said, eventually, after finishing the "a."

"No," she said, hesitating. "Are you?"

"No."

"Your parents will be worried, won't they?"

"Yeah. I guess so."

They fell silent again. There was the far-off sound of an engine, a constant buzzing, as if there were an old fan on the other side of the wall, its blades spinning tirelessly.

"It's strange, isn't it?"

"What?"

"Being here, now, the two of us. It's strange."

"Yeah."

He turned his head, looked at her. She felt his gaze. She felt, too, that her ear was growing hot. As if Rodrigo's pupils were hot coals. But she didn't turn her head. She carried on staring upward. Ceilings are so flat. Smooth, simple, nothing interesting about them at all.

"Where are we going to go tomorrow? Do you know?"

María couldn't help it: she rotated her whole body around and moved onto her side, facing him.

"No. But I still have to leave."

They looked into each other's eyes. How much can fit inside a look? What is love or desire when you are nine, ten years old? What does the body feel like, what does wanting feel like? Writing always comes later. The story never describes what takes place, but instead what is remembered.

"What are you thinking about?"

"Nothing."

"Do you wish you hadn't come?"

"No. I told you. I'm coming with you."

"What, then? What are you thinking about?"

Rodrigo hesitated again. He was scared that another letter would stick to the roof of his mouth.

"I don't know. I was thinking . . ." He stopped, took a while to find the word. "Shouldn't we . . . shouldn't we kiss?"

And immediately he felt ridiculous, silly, cheesy. He wished he could tear apart with his hands the scene that had just played out before them. But María smiled. And she kissed him.

For the first time since the arrival of Andreína and her troops, evening in the apartment felt relatively calm. Only the television remained switched on, tuned to the official state channel, almost until sunrise. The three women sat in front of the screen, melancholic and engrossed. They couldn't believe it.

Andreína sat in silence, in a chair next to the dining-room table. Tatiana was busy collecting her personal possessions. She had called the police. They told her that in order to report somebody missing she had to wait twenty-four hours. She had tried to sleep but, as soon as she began to slip into unconsciousness, a persistent anguish would immediately wake her up. Suddenly dawn arrived and she had no idea if she had actually slept or not, even for just a few minutes. The only thing the night had left her with any certainty was a bitter taste in her mouth. Not a minute went by without her thinking about Rodrigo. She felt so guilty. She allowed herself to be seized by anxiety and grief.

She also dreamed about Fredy, or perhaps she only imagined him. Her husband, who had disappeared in Cuba, disappeared into the depths of the sea. She saw him shirtless, with a bottle of rum in his hand, stumbling along the seafront where green waves were surging, like long seaweed fingers smashing against the rocks. Then she saw him, or perhaps she dreamed or imagined it, drowned in a bay. The sea was smooth, like a tablecloth with no creases. Dark and smooth. The only thing that

stood out was Fredy's head. With his eyes closed and his
mouth open. His purple lips were trembling slightly.

The next day, the two women almost bumped into one
another in the hallway.

Tatiana was dragging two large suitcases behind her.
Her features were arranged differently somehow. Her
expression was a combination of sadness and intense
hatred. Each pupil contained an *I hope you rot in hell*, and
cheerless derision wavered in her smile. That was all she
could do to deal with her defeat. Andreína looked back
at her blankly.

"My brother will come sometime this week to collect
the rest of our things."

Andreína put up no resistance, she said that wouldn't
be a problem.

"You're a bitch. A piece of shit."

Andreína said nothing.

"All of this will come back to haunt you one day."

Andreína did not respond. Tatiana hauled the suitcases toward the door.

Deep down, both of them were too exhausted to
resume the fight. The end was just like the beginning.
They had come back to words. After everything that
had happened, they were forced to speak, to negotiate.
Tatiana left and Andreína closed the door, unusually
gently. The door swung slowly shut, almost despite itself.
The tiny sound of the lock clicking into place boomed
in her ears. The other three women were sound asleep.
Andreína wanted to shout, release a scream that would
echo across the valley. But instead she stood there in
silence. Without peeling her back off the door, she let
herself slide slowly down to the floor. The cold granite

against her buttocks felt like a blessing too. The morning had delivered a miracle, she thought.

A few hours later, the telephone rang. The day had maintained the same atmosphere as the previous afternoon. It was one of mourning. A painful astonishment that didn't know exactly how to absorb the news, how to accept it. Virginia had woken up and was making coffee. The other two were still asleep. Andreína told her what had happened: Tatiana had finally left that morning. Virginia didn't seem particularly happy about it but she said oh good, or something like that, she was talking very quietly. Then she pointed out that they would have left on Tuesday anyway. Their job was done.

Andreína nodded. Then a silence settled between them.

Virginia said they would leave early. That they wanted to go to the funeral.

Today is a sacred day, she added.

And that's when the telephone rang.

It was Fredy Lecuna. He had just landed. He was still inside the airplane, on his feet, in the aisle, waiting to disembark. Virginia, who had answered, told him drily that Tatiana no longer lived there. She hung up. Fredy was agitated. He hadn't slept, he had a terrible hangover. He still hadn't wholly recovered from the vile rum and the excellent surprise on the night of his farewell.

"Throughout the history of humankind, everything has depended on the quality of the resources," Omar had said, after taking his first sip of alcohol. "With this," he had added, "Nero would have burnt the entire empire to the ground."

Fredy would actually have preferred no celebration at all, he just wanted to get off the island as soon as possible. He was, by now, completely overwhelmed and desperate to go home. He had been feeling worse and worse, drowning in the marriage farce which hadn't even delivered the journalistic reward he had been hoping for. He sensed it would be impossible to arrive in Caracas and sit before his wife and explain to her that he had married a Cuban woman and that he was tangled up in the process of getting her legally off the island. Would Tatiana believe him when he told her there had never been anything between him and the Cuban? Would she trust him? And the publishers? His deadline had come and gone, Chávez was dead, and he was coming back from Havana without having finished writing his great best seller.

Halfway through the party, Aylín suddenly grabbed him and dragged him toward the room where they slept. Fredy briefly feared that the rum had stimulated his wife's libido, that Aylín wanted to wish him a more sensuous farewell. He began to recite, in a reprimanding tone, all the agreements they had made regarding any intimacy between them. Waiting in the narrow bedroom was the paramedic who for so long had delayed the supposed handover of confidential information. Aylín demanded he give Fredy what he had brought. The man seemed nervous and stiff, as if he had somehow been forced to be there, to act in this way. He offered Fredy a blue folder that contained some papers. He told him that inside were the results of the last tests they had carried out on the Commander. There was also a detailed medical report, signed by the medical committee that had attended him.

"Everything they never wanted to say is in there," he exclaimed, his voice hoarse.

Fredy Lecuna had to pay, of course. He also had to say

thank you to Aylín and commit to continuing with the marital process. But this fleeting and somewhat evasive meeting, which occurred at the last minute, under the spell of the vile rum, meant his entire trip and his book project had taken a 180-degree turn. He felt excited, his motivation was back, it was vigorous. He thought that now he had good reason to ask the publisher to push the deadline back another week or two, and he could confront Tatiana and fix everything he had damaged over the last few months.

"Are you Fredy Lecuna?"

The journalist hadn't even completely disembarked from the airplane, he hadn't taken a single step when three people surrounded him. They were dressed in plain clothes but it was obvious they were policemen. Only one of them was wearing sunglasses. He was the only one not wearing a tie. But all three of them had the same confidence in their expressions that comes with carrying a hidden weapon.

Fredy said yes, but with very little conviction. It was a crooked, evasive yes.

The man wearing the sunglasses approached him, leaned forward so his face was close to Fredy's, and whispered in an unmistakable Cuban accent:

"Come with us for a moment, please."

When he heard the doorbell ring, Sanabria thought it was Tatiana. He hadn't heard the buzzer from the main entrance to the building, so it couldn't be anyone from outside. He imagined, happily, that Rodrigo had appeared and he felt hugely relieved. He was eating a mandarin in front of the television, hearing about all the preparations for the ostentatious funeral rites that were beginning that day. As soon as the doorbell rang he leaped up, his hand reaching the latch in a matter of seconds. He opened the door and found himself face-to-face with a young woman, very white, brown hair, green eyes, and a shy smile playing on her lips. The concierge was standing next to her, gesturing toward her with a certain degree of pride.

"It's the American journalist, she's come to see you. She told me you were expecting her."

Sanabria's face contracted, suddenly transforming into a frown, a question mark wrinkling his brow. The concierge left immediately and Sanabria could do nothing but invite Madeleine Butler inside.

They sat down in front of the television. He offered her a cup of coffee and she declined.

"Water?"

"No, thank you."

They exchanged two or three innocuous phrases, pure pleasantries. Together they watched a new official advertisement about the commemorations. Soon they would be moving Chávez's coffin from the military hospital to the military academy, where his remains would lie in state.

"You know why I'm here," the journalist finally said. She was tactful, but not timid.

The sound of the telephone ringing prevented the silence from stretching out uneasily. Sanabria felt intimidated and uncomfortable. He got up far too quickly and clumsily grabbed the telephone. He made an apologetic gesture as he backed away slightly and said hello. It was his brother. Sanabria was expecting a different voice. He was constantly longing for Tatiana to appear with good news about Rodrigo. But no. It was Antonio, asking if he was watching the news. Sanabria's eyes instinctively darted toward the television.

"I just hope they don't fuck this up," muttered Antonio.

Sanabria didn't know what or who he was talking about.

"You know. Fireworks. Music, throwing a party. Everyone in the opposition wants that."

"I'm not so sure," said Sanabria.

His brother told him that Vladimir had finally appeared. Sanabria smiled courteously at the journalist. He made another gesture, excusing himself. She made a similar movement in return, suggesting that she didn't mind, that she could wait.

"He's in the military academy," Antonio continued, with a hint of pride. "They named him chief of one of the commissions in charge of the Eternal Commander's funerals."

Sanabria replied in brief monosyllables, ambiguous expressions that wouldn't mean anything to his visitor. Antonio explained that Vladimir was very close to the vice president, it was his understanding that his future was looking important and full of responsibilities during the new era of the revolution.

Sanabria went into the kitchen and picked up a mandarin.

Antonio was quiet for a few seconds.

"Vladimir asked me to call you," his brother said finally, his tone suddenly more serious.

Sanabria felt once again a cold and sudden jolt at the center of his back.

"What about?" he stammered, as he moved back toward the living room.

"He wanted me to tell you not to give the box to the American woman."

Sanabria stopped.

"What?" The word flew out of his mouth. He couldn't catch it.

The journalist seemed a little surprised to hear him shout, but she kept her eyes firmly on the television.

"We want you to return the box, Miguel."

Sanabria suddenly felt dizzy.

"Why?" he managed to ask.

He sunk into a corner of the living room, near the window. He felt nervous, confused. His brother's use of the plural had left him short of breath. He tried to understand what was going on, what was happening exactly. Antonio told him he couldn't give him an explanation.

"Vladimir and I have decided to forgive and forget. He told me everything. I told him that he had made a big mistake trusting you."

His voice sounded dry. Very dry. Sanabria felt a lump of saliva crawling across the back of his tongue.

"I'm your brother, Antonio."

"Yes," he said. "But you're also a counterrevolution-ary," he added.

Suddenly, a silence seeped in, a silence that became more rigid with every second that went by. Sanabria was holding the telephone in his hand but he was looking at Madeleine Butler, who was still sitting down, almost in the same position, waiting patiently.

"I don't have it," he said. As if he was speaking to both of them at the same time. "I don't have the mobile Vladimir gave me anymore. I've lost the videos."

Cecilia had to find a locksmith in order to open the door and get into the apartment. When the lock gave way, various neighbors were with her. They couldn't believe that the girl had spent so many weeks living alone in the apartment. Not one of them had noticed. They never went out, they kept themselves to themselves, one said. Another added: There was nothing in the news, how were we supposed to know she had died? The lady who lived below them remembered finding the girl in the stairwell once, and that María had told her that her mother was unwell, resting. Cecilia felt obliged to tell the whole story, her tone somewhere between amazed and indignant. She was furious. She couldn't imagine why María wouldn't open the door. She didn't understand what was going on.

She was the first to go into the living room. She was surprised by how tidy and clean everything was. The neighbors came in eagerly behind her, gazing around them inquisitively. Soon they were all going around in circles. There was clearly nobody home. The girl had gone.

"How strange," someone said, pointing. "She left the television on."

They all looked. The screen, mute, was showing the images of the ceremony taking place in the city. A funeral cortège was advancing through the crowd with some difficulty. There, on top of the long black pickup truck, was the coffin.

They knew exactly who he was, where he had been, and what he had done. With whom he had spoken, the places he had gone, what he had spent his money on. They had information about Aylín, her family, their wedding, the details of the paperwork they had filed requesting permission to leave the island. They knew everything and they made sure to tell him in the worst possible way: with absolute civility.

They also knew, of course, about the folder an informant had given him just before he left the island. They wanted to see it, they wanted to check any papers the journalist had received. Fredy denied everything. Later, he admitted everything, but only half-heartedly. Then, faced with the first hint of the possible use of violence, he admitted, or rather confirmed, everything. He showed them the folder and the material it contained, he offered them a comprehensive story, including unnecessary details about his stay and his inquiries in Havana. The policemen were satisfied and, after a brief, hushed exchange, they left the small room where they had been interrogating him. Fredy asked himself what would happen next. He quickly came to several conclusions. They couldn't detain him. He hadn't committed any crime. They couldn't stop him from writing, either. You can't prohibit writing. You can censor it, change it, control it, avoid it, but you cannot erase it.

Writing is the same as illness: it is inevitable.

Fredy Lecuna didn't have time to keep thinking. The door opened and a man of about sixty appeared; dressed elegantly but informally, he was accompanied by a younger man who had long hair and the look of a university professor about him. They didn't even introduce themselves. One remained standing while the other sat down in front of the journalist.

"You're in trouble," he said.

Lecuna produced a series of ambivalent gestures, unthinkingly.

"One of the cops just told me they found cocaine in your luggage."

At first the journalist laughed, he thought it was a joke. Then, shocked, he protested, said it was a cheap trick, that they couldn't do something like that to him. The two men remained silent. Lecuna began to feel afraid.

"We have a proposal for you," said the man who was sitting down.

"What would that be?"

"We are going to give you a hundred thousand dollars."

Fredy Lecuna wanted to laugh again but the joke was stuck fast in his stomach. His mouth would not shut.

"So that I don't write the book?" he managed to stammer.

The man smiled, looked up, and glanced sideways at the one who looked like a university professor, as if they had made a bet just before they came in. Then he looked back at the journalist again.

"No, just the opposite. We are going to give you a hundred thousand dollars so that you do write the book."

Lecuna looked at him. He was speechless. But it was obvious the man was serious. He was sitting there in front of Fredy, a sardonic smile on his face, waiting for an answer.

"I don't understand," he said, trying to buy time.

They explained: the idea was to keep everything the same, the same plan, the same publisher, but writing a different kind of book, another direction, a direction more in line with the interests of the revolution, the defense of the motherland, and also the defense of the life and memory of the Commander.

"This is a matter concerning the stability of the country," they said at a certain point.

They could provide whatever information he needed, and they were insistent that the book should seem like an autonomous piece of work, an impartial investigative exercise by an independent journalist.

"You want me to create propaganda that doesn't seem like propaganda?" Lecuna asked, somewhat more confident, daring to use a little irony in his tone.

The men looked at one another again.

The journalist remembered the supposed cocaine they said they had found in his luggage. He also remembered the political police officers, the Cuban in the sunglasses. He imagined them on the other side of the door, waiting.

"It's a good deal, Lecuna. Think about it."

It didn't take very long for Andreína Mijares to understand the meaning of the look on Tatiana's face when she had said goodbye. She began to realize when she went into the bathroom and saw the glass door was shattered. The mirror had also been struck in one corner with a blunt object and was cracked. In the boy's room, the curtain was in shreds, as if the night before they had been attacked with scissors. In one corner, on the carpet, there was an enormous stain. It smelled like nail varnish remover mixed with some other substance. Little by little, she discovered the extent of her ex-tenant's revenge. Tatiana had done, in her own way, the same thing they had. She had spent her last night there carrying out a painstaking job of destruction. Nothing was left standing. In the end, nothing belonged to anyone.

Virginia, Mildred, and Dusty left a little after midday. Andreína told them they could take whatever they wanted. Mildred took a table lamp with a blue lampshade and Chinese drawings on the porcelain base. Dusty chose an art deco blown-glass ashtray. Virginia took the remaining half of the money and said thank you.

"See? It went well, didn't it?" she said. "In the end, they always go," she declared. "Nobody can take it."

And then she said they should stay in touch. She explained that the three of them sometimes worked on bigger projects, on invasions of abandoned or unsold buildings.

"Once, by way of payment, they gave us two apartments," she said. "We sold them afterward for affordable prices," she added. "Who knows? Something like this could happen again and you or someone you know might be interested in buying an apartment from us."

Andreína nodded, without saying a word.

The women left in a hurry. They wanted to see if they could go and join the funeral procession. The three of them said goodbye and gave her a hug. Dusty winked at her.

"Think about what has happened to you," said Virginia just before she left. "Really use your head. See the truth. The revolution protects you lot, too. The revolution is for everyone."

As soon as they reached Paseo de Los Próceres, the

crowd surrounded the vehicle. Not even the heavy security detail could get the funeral cortège to move any faster. The sun was high in the sky, radiating a yellow and humid, decisive heat. Sanabria was sitting in front of the television. Still sitting next to him was Madeleine Butler. She had accepted a glass of water and was softly sipping the liquid, without taking her eyes off the television.

Antonio hadn't believed him. He thought the story about hiding the telephone in the neighbor's son's backpack was bizarre, unbelievable in fact. His brother had become sarcastic, rude. He thought it was all a trick, a ruse so he could keep the videos, in order to use them with conspiratorial motives, perhaps. He shouted at him. He threatened him. And so Sanabria hung up. He switched off his phone and left the landline off the hook. Then he served himself a whiskey on the rocks. The journalist said she would prefer a glass of water.

"Would you like a mandarin?"

The journalist shook her head.

They were both quiet for a moment, watching the television. They spoke without looking at one another. Sanabria wanted to get an idea of how much she grasped, if she had heard and understood the conversation he had had on the telephone. She had an inkling but she didn't fully comprehend what was going on. Sanabria explained in detail. On the screen, a mass of people moved like a caterpillar around the coffin. The cameras zoomed in on the people's devastated, tearful faces.

"So," Madeleine suddenly asked, "did you watch the videos?"

Sanabria looked at her. She seemed embarrassed. As

if asking the question was an uncomfortable duty, a rule she had no choice but to comply with.

"Yes."

The journalist raised the glass to her lips. She let the silence do its work.

"They were very short," Sanabria added. "And very bad quality."

"But could you see anything or not?"

Sanabria moved his head. He hesitated for a moment, while Madeleine waited expectantly, her body tense.

"Yes."

The journalist squirmed in her seat, brought her hands together, it was clear she was increasingly anxious for an answer.

"I saw a very sick man, a human being, vulnerable and desperate. Like any terminally ill patient."

"That was it?" she asked, a little disappointed.

Sanabria took another sip, and sighed.

"I imagine they filmed him before the operation."

Madeleine Butler didn't blink. She kept watching him, her gaze steady, holding her breath.

"He was crying. He was in a great deal of pain. And he said he didn't want to die. He was begging for help, for them to not let him die."

On the television, a woman, her eyes filled with tears, raised her hands toward the sky.

"It's a horrible video, shocking, I don't quite know how to explain."

Madeleine looked at him pleadingly. She wanted him to keep talking.

"Did he say anything else?"

"He was weak, fragile, terrified. He was crying.

Complaining. He was very afraid of death. Like anyone would be."

"But Chávez wasn't just anybody, was he?" the journalist whispered.

"Chávez had cancer," Sanabria pointed out.

Fredy Lecuna handed them the folder, and in return he received a series of medical reports, including the written testimonies of a few nurses and doctors who had supposedly treated Chávez in Havana. They also gave him a $30,000 advance, in hundred-dollar notes, stacked inside a yellow envelope. The journalist left without a word.

The same officials who had stopped him were waiting outside. They escorted him back to immigration control. While he was waiting in the queue, he thought about how everything had changed so drastically in only a few hours. Who was he, really? Had he perhaps lost all remaining ties to himself, to his own life, to what he had been up until this moment? What had happened? How had he gotten here? He gripped the envelope more tightly under his arm. He thought the money felt light. That dollars didn't weigh all that much.

Moving the coffin from the military hospital to the military academy, where Hugo Chávez's body lay in state, took more than seven hours. The fact that the point of departure and arrival were both military institutions was the perfect metaphor for his existence. That was who Chávez was: a soldier. That was his nature, his rationale, and his perception of the world. He had faith in the uniform, not in diversity. He believed in obedience, not agreement. A few months after the first time he won the presidency, he said so: "I don't believe in any party, not even in my own. I believe in the military, which is where I was trained." His coffin's route followed a path from the military hospital, where he had died, to the armed forces school where he was trained, where he had found his true calling. Two essentially masculine spaces, ruled by secrecy, by the vertical rigidity of men who dress exactly the same way every day. Between these two points were the others, the crowd, the public.

María and Rodrigo were there, on the edge of the sidewalk, watching the procession of people pass by. They were each carrying a backpack. María also had a small suitcase on wheels. Rodrigo's small backpack dangled from his left shoulder.

Never before had they seen up close so many people at the same time. There were all kinds of people. Women dressed in red, crying; young people and old; soldiers, policemen, civil servants. There were also many journalists, men and women with cameras and microphones, foreign correspondents. There were people from the church, priests and pastors, bands, trying to create a harmony in the middle of the commotion. It was an irregular and enormous tide. Like a rally but with a different ending. After the trajectory, the leader would not be able to speak.

On the screen, the crowd seemed even bigger, as if it had been stuffed into the frame, as if the image could barely fit.

"And the second video?" asked Madeleine Butler, with the same apprehensive, respectful expression she had maintained the entire time.

Sanabria hesitated for a moment, squeezing a mandarin tightly in his right hand. Perhaps he thought that there wasn't much point in all of this anymore, that everything had inevitably come to an end.

"The second video was more or less the same," Sanabria told her. "Perhaps he seemed a little more pathetic. He had difficulty speaking, got mixed up. He was probably under the effect of some kind of sedative. He spoke about a daughter he had on the island of Margarita and, then, suddenly, he would say something about the country, and then he would start to cry again. And he was shouting about wanting to live. And he would beg them to please save him."

Madeleine listened, impassive.

"I suppose they don't want anyone to see Chávez that way. Especially not now."

Madeleine Butler looked at the images on the television, then returned her gaze to Sanabria.

"Why?" she asked.

For a moment, Dr. Sanabria was lost in thought. As if he hadn't heard the question.

"Because gods do not have bodies," he replied without looking at her. "Gods do not shout out from pain, they do not bleed from the anus, they do not cry. Gods do not beg to be saved. Gods do not die slowly and in agony."

Madeleine glanced toward the bookshelves. She noticed the cigar box, balanced on top of a row of books. She pointed at it.

"Is that the box? Can I look at it?"

As soon as she shut the door, Andreína Mijares noticed a different echo: the sound of the closing door shuddered in the air and then continued jumping softly around the entire apartment. It sunk in that she was alone. After all this time, she was finally alone and on her territory. She walked around slowly, calmly visiting every part of the apartment. Everything was filthy. Her home was devastated. All the furniture was dirty or broken, the floor and the walls were disgusting, there was leftover food and rubbish everywhere.

The telephone rang.

Andreína did not pick up. She was silent, standing in the doorway of the kitchen, looking around at the wreckage of the disaster. She had finally done it. This was her victory.

The television was on. Accompanying the images of the funeral cortège was Chávez's voice, singing the national anthem.

Tatiana had asked a friend to take her in, a university professor who had written several children's books. Her name was Irene, and she was a shy, reserved woman. She was the one who opened the door to Fredy.

"She's in the shower," she said. "You can wait for her here if you like."

She invited him to come through to the study. Then she asked if he would like some coffee. Fredy said yes and she left, closing the door behind her.

It was a square room, without windows. There were bookshelves all the way up two of the walls, packed with books. On the wall facing the door was a desk, a simple glass table, on top of which was a computer. Fredy noticed a small piece of paper stuck to the wall, placed at the exact height of the eyes of whomever was sitting at the desk. It was ocher-colored and bore a handwritten sentence:

"Nothing corrupts a man so deeply as writing a book."—Rex Stout.

He heard distant voices. He imagined Tatiana and Irene talking in the kitchen. He pushed his suitcase over next to the bookshelves, leaving the envelope full of money on top of it. He also tried to tidy his hair. He had only exchanged a few brief words with Tatiana. On his fourth attempt, she had finally answered her phone.

"Hello! It's me! I'm here! What happened?" Fredy had let all these words tumble out at once, in a nervous and uncertain order.

Tatiana responded sparingly. She told him she was staying at Irene's house. That they needed to talk. Nothing else.

He was surprised when he saw her. She had just come out of the shower, and she looked drawn. She looked almost ill. As if she had lost two or three kilos and hadn't slept in several days. He wanted to wrap his arms around her. But the look on Tatiana's face was an impenetrable barrier. Fredy lowered his head immediately.

"Forgive me," he whispered.

Tatiana looked at him. In silence.

"What happened?" he asked, taking one step forward.

"Everything, Fredy."

Feeling worse with every second that went by, he moved toward the suitcase and picked up the envelope.

"Don't worry, my love, I have good news, I promise!" he exclaimed, offering her the envelope.

Tatiana didn't move. She kept looking at him with the same expression.

"There is no more good news, Fredy. Why don't you ask me about Rodrigo?"

"So the boy ran away from home?" said the American journalist, now on her feet, next to the bookshelves, picking up the box with both her hands.

"Yes. In fact, his family doesn't even live here anymore."

"You mean you don't know how to find him?"

"Exactly."

The journalist unclasped the small latch.

"And what do you think will happen now with the revolution?" she asked, as if to stretch the conversation out a bit further, as she managed finally to open the box.

"This is not a revolution. This is just a farce," muttered Sanabria without taking his eyes off the screen.

The journalist dipped her fingers into the box.

"It's empty," said Sanabria.

Madeleine Butler turned around and looked at him, confused. After everything he had told her, it was obvious it would be empty. She didn't understand why he had said that. But then she saw him. Sanabria's eyes were still fixed on the screen. His right hand was raised. His fingers were pointing at the television.

"There is nobody in it," he said.

The journalist went back to the sofa and sat down beside him, still not fully comprehending his words. They both looked at the screen: the images showed the coffin, secured to the top of the long black vehicle, surrounded by a febrile throng.

"There is no way his body can be inside there," whispered Sanabria. "It wouldn't hold up for so long, especially not with this heat."

The horde looked like a hot sea, wet, injured. It was a red procession, full of pain, wrapped in inescapable sadness. It moved so slowly that it didn't seem to be advancing at all, it only swayed, coming and going, with no particular destination, around an empty box.

"How do you feel?"
        "I'm not sure. Everything is strange."
        "Do you want to go back?"
        "It's too late for that."
        "So, what are we going to do? Where are we going?"